M000315460

Mrs. Alworth

Tim Castano

Mrs. Alworth

COPYRIGHT © 2021 by Tim Castano
COVER AND BOOK DESIGN by Alexandru Oprescu

All rights reserved. Published by New Meridian, part of the non-profit organization New Meridian Arts, 2021.

No part of this publication may be reproduced, or stored in a retrieval system, or transmitted in any form or by any means, electronic, mechanical, photocopying, or otherwise, without written permission of the publisher, except in the case of brief quotations in reviews. For information regarding permission, write to newmeridianarts1@gmail.com

LIBRARY OF CONGRESS CATALOGING-IN-PUBLICATION DATA
Mrs. Alworth
Authored by Tim Castano
ISBN: 9781734383584
LCCN: 2021941609

For Greg, Chris and John

Contents

CHAPTER ONE

Amanda

The iodine clock reaction.

When I first saw him, the thought in my head: the iodine clock reaction, the experiment from years ago in school. The teacher had transformed a clear glass of water into a rich, stormy blue. My classmates gasped and giggled, as if a magic trick. To me, science could explain magic or what some had come to mistake as magic.

Whatever I felt when I looked at Orest Alworth, my mind ran immediately to the iodine clock reaction.

CHAPTER TWO

Amanda

The next person to check *Anomalies and Curiosities of Medicine* out of the Newark Public Library might see my name on the card inside the cover.

This person might wonder what happened to Amanda Bannon.

I might be dead.

More than "might," to be honest. And I almost always am honest.

I had read the card when I took out the book in early October of 1922. It last went out in August of 1916. Six years. In six more years, I would be twenty-five. Twenty-five might be too much to ask. But I would ask, because I already had received more than promised. The doctors did not think I would live to see thirteen. Last month, I celebrated my nineteenth birthday. What do doctors know?

On my fifteenth birthday, I insisted my family stop referring to my advancing age as a miracle.

"It's science, not a miracle," I told them. "Don't insult me with miracles."

They laughed the way people do when they have spoken about you behind your back.

"Look who's so serious," said Elizabeth, my sister.

"I live with death inside of me," I said, about the closest I ever have come to writing a line of poetry. The comment stunned them silent, uncomfortable, which I enjoyed. But I could not stop there. I had to press, to inflict a little pain, so they would remember, because pain almost always makes you remember. "And so do all of you."

Out of their mouths, in unison, came that click-sigh sound: the tongue peeling fast off the roof of the mouth, puffing out as a judgmental breath. Then, they lied to themselves, making it seem as if I had gone too far in front of Catherine, only about nine at the time. If honest, they would have had to admit how I had gone too far for each of them. The unavoidable, a bit too much: *We'll all be dead one day*. Easier to lash out than swallow down that truth.

So interesting, how family members leave impressions on one another. Not like those first impressions of strangers, all dynamite and nitroglycerin, blasting fast, permanent craters in our minds. Maybe more like a volcano, not that I know much about volcanoes, other than what I have read. The magma builds and heats under the surface, perhaps leaking out as steam. An incident triggers an eruption. The anger and frustration and irritation spill out, ultimately cooling and hardening into new terrain. My fifteenth birthday felt like an eruption, their impressions of me cooling and hardening afterward.

Elizabeth, eighteen: *This is why I never can talk to her.*
Joseph, my father: *This is why I prefer the other two.*
Margaret, my mother: *This is why she is so difficult.*
Even Catherine, so young: *This is why I'm afraid of her.*
Whatever their impressions, whatever the cost, worth it to me. They never again mentioned miracles.

Neither did *Anomalies and Curiosities of Medicine.* Too heavy for miracles. Truth weighs more than fiction, I believe. Novels were slender, pretty things with big type for slender, pretty girls with small voices, like Elizabeth. My books were weighty, stretching forearm tendons and hurting elbow joints when I lifted them. Plain covers with serviceable fonts meant to pack in as many words as possible. I liked how the hard, waxed lips of the spines jammed red crevices in my abdomen when I read in bed each night, the soreness the last sensation before I fell asleep. Pain almost always makes you remember.

I already had reached page three hundred and sixty-seven: "The preponderance of centenarians of the supposed weaker sex has led to the revival of some amusing theories tending to explain this phenomenon." This sentence, worth remembering. I appreciated how the author described the theories as "amusing." Condescension understood by an ambitious few. And I counted myself among those few. "Don't be so condescending," my mother sometimes would tell me, which sounded like, "Don't be so good at what you do." Made no sense to me.

I had earned my condescension. Entrance into an exclusive society, with fees paid by lugging heavy, plain books to and from the library, to and from my house, to and from my job. I liked the image I must have imprinted: gangly arms wrapped around a massive volume, a tiny insect stumbling while carrying a giant leaf.

I liked the thud when I dropped the books on my desk at Saint Barnabas Hospital. The sound announced my arrival to coworkers, who would not bother to look up. Their disregard, just jealousy, since I might one day have a career beyond signing in patients and handing over files.

Did I condescend? Yes, of course. But they patronized.

"What are you reading that for?" asked one of the other receptionists during my first week on the job.

I knew enough not to give her a straight answer, not then. I said, "I like to read." Could not tell her the real reason. Could not say, "I'm studying to become a doctor," because she and others would tease me, start calling me "Doctor Bannon" as some sort of joke. And I could not let the idea become a joke. Which is not to say I did not look forward to some fun.

I imagine a scene in the not-so-distant future. I would enter an examination room to find a family, one a patient, maybe a young girl with her parents, not unlike how my family must have appeared. The father probably would tell me, "We're waiting for the doctor." I would get to say, "I am the doctor." Then, I would observe. Disbelief and stuttering confusion from the father. Maybe embarrassment in the mother. In the girl, a hope she might have met the person who could explain why she was in that hospital. All so satisfying to me. All worth the sore elbow joints and red-abdomen crevices and jealous coworkers. All worth the boring folders and charts and endless questions from the newly admitted about where to go, how long to wait. All worth inhaling the disinfectant the crews slopped on the floors three times each day, so visitors would think they had stepped into the Northeast's cleanest facility. By four o'clock in the afternoon, the end of the shift, my eyelashes flapped so heavy and slow in those phenol fumes, my brain so drowsy, I wished I could place my head on the desk and awake in my bed back home. That type of miracle, I would have welcomed.

Without it, I had to walk from High Street to Pennsylvania Avenue in an evening already cold and dark. I had charted every possible route between the hospital and my house. Some took longer than others. I often would choose the longer ones at the end of the day, to delay. To delay having to help Catherine with her homework. To delay having to mediate one of those useless debates about how much Newark was changing, for the better or the worse. I sometimes would go to Lincoln Park and sit, waiting to see if my father would notice me on his way from the precinct on Court and Washington. A few nights, he passed right in front of me. I would follow him quietly, until the moment I could approach fast from behind and yell in his ear, "Hello, Dad." A police Captain does not appreciate being startled.

Against my father's wishes, I occasionally would wander around the Coast, the city's cluster of night-clubs and less-legitimate establishments. Some described it as lively. Others dusted off words from the Old Testament: wicked, depraved, iniquitous. The musicians often would rehearse with the doors open in the late afternoons. Small crowds would gather outside the venues, the stop-start songs reaching the streets as free, spontaneous concerts. I once stood outside of Randolph's, listening for a few minutes. An older man said to me, "You've any idea you're being treated to James P. Johnson, young lady? One of the best ever."

No James P. Johnson or Randolph's on this day. Too cold. Too dark. Too tired. Only the most direct path, however dull. The loose tissue in my cheeks rattled with each foot plant along the sidewalk. My nose dribbled in the chill. Too dozy to rub it clean. The rattle in my chest slowed me down every few blocks. So that no one from my family would see me cough, I sucked in and held a lungful of air before I turned onto our street. Made it to the front steps and sent out a cloud of carbon dioxide and germs into the neighborhood. Once through the door, in the form of my mother, regret greeted me. Regret for having not stayed out later, maybe indefinitely.

"Your father wants all of us at dinner tonight," she said. "He has a guest."

"All of us? Elizabeth and Tom?"

"Even Aunt Cecilia."

The name alone, emphasis.

"Aunt Cecilia? Who is it?"

"Didn't say. Only wanted all of us here. You'll help me put out the places. The good ones."

Trading folders on one side of town for forks on another did not seem like a favorable exchange. I had learned years ago, though, obedience would get me up to my room faster than an argument.

"Another young officer?" I asked as I plunked down plates. "You already married off Elizabeth. No reason for Dad to bring one of them around."

"Didn't say."

"Mayor Breidenbach? Bishop O'Connor?"

"Ah-man-dah," she said, pronouncing hard each syllable. Her exasperation, more for my father than for me, if honest. As usual, he had given little information and expected action, his sly way of reinforcing some unwritten patriarchal power dynamic. My mother, ever in disagreement, went along. She always went along. I knew this bothered her. Why I kept probing. So, yes, I probably deserved some of her exasperation.

In truth, Mayor, Bishop, I did not care. Any guest would do. Someone else to disrupt our monotonous, how-was-your-day exchanges. A guest also made me more a part of the family, as opposed to set me apart from the family. (Sister Mary Rose always stressed the distinction between *apart* and *a part* for the slower girls as Saint Vincent's.) Growing up, the five of us at a meal, I felt like the guest. Each of them—Dad, Mom,

Elizabeth, Catherine—could look across the table and see at least the hint of a reflection. Wide-jawed, brown-eyed and chestnut hair, Dad and Catherine. Blonde, green-eyed and fine-boned, Mom and Elizabeth. Me? Slate-gray eyes dug up from some quarry. A head covered in an earth-colored tangle framing uninteresting proportions and slopes. If only my nose were larger or crooked, I would tell myself, at least I would stand out.

When joined at dinner by Aunt Cecilia—a tower of fading auburn hair atop a wiry, porcelain doll—or by horn-rimmed, perfectly parted Tom, I belonged a little more among the Bannon family. Or I belonged with the outsiders. Either way, I belonged.

The dining room, finally ready for the pageant, with pressed tablecloth and high-gloss china. Against the walls soon would bounce chair honks and the shuttle of dishes, Elizabeth's end-of-sentence tonal lifts and my mother's rare, unnerving use of the word "shall." Across the gold-and-olive-striped wallpaper, Aunt Cecilia would splatter decorum with an inappropriate comment or two. I would sigh and shrug.

Up to my bedroom before the arrival, I sat in the windowsill, my back against one side and, with knees bent, feet against the other. I pressed my left cheek fully to the glass, Pennsylvania Avenue's night rush a beating-heart echo in half my head. The silhouettes of the nearly identical houses. The humming pattern of pedestrians. Slowly, the scene absorbed me, the shadows of lamps and bookends expanding across the walls.

CHAPTER THREE

Elizabeth

People notice me.

I notice almost everything.

I would not call it a gift. More like a skill, because I had worked at noticing for so long. Since childhood, hours and hours recording moods and postures and expressions. No one thought I paid such close attention, but I did. I think a relationship exists between the effort one devotes to an act and the pride one derives from performing the act. I am proud of how well I notice.

People notice me so intently, they overlook what I might notice. They do not appreciate what I might see. I think this was why I fell in love with Tom. Not that he noticed me, because a lot of men did. They still do. No, Tom cared about what I noticed. After all, he looked only somewhat like the man I envisioned I might marry: lanky and reserved and safe and gentle. The more he listened, though, "somewhat" became "exactly."

An accountant with Prudential, he told me on one of our first outings, "Insurance men are taking over the city. We've got most of the offices on Market and

Broad now." Misguided and charming, how he thought a woman actually might find this point at all alluring.

"I read Newark is as busy as any other city in the country, even Manhattan," I said, if only to keep our conversation moving.

"Really? Where did you read that? I would love to learn more."

He meant it, too. His eyes, earnest and inviting. Not the feigned interest other men showed me, pretend fascination that surely would have flickered after they achieved whatever outcome they desired. No, Tom meant it then and has meant it since. That discussion might have been the moment, the moment I decided to give him a chance. And he did not waste his chance. I knew he would continue to care about what I would notice, even after people stopped noticing me, which would happen. Always does.

I still enjoy noticing my husband more than a year into our marriage. I noticed that when he shook Orest Alworth's hand the night my father first brought him home for dinner, Tom made sure the ligaments between their thumbs and index fingers met with a friendly aggression, the way men do. I noticed him in my family's living room the evening when Aunt Cecilia said to Orest, "Never heard of Gene Tunney? He's going to be champion one day. Mark my words. Think I've been to all his fights in Newark. Two bouts a couple of years ago. In August, saw him beat Charley Weinert. Tommy took me."

Sitting on the couch, Tom glanced up from the evening paper. Shut his eyes and folded his bottom lip into his mouth. I could see the distressing memory play in his head: the expletives Aunt Cecilia hurled at the ring, the senior manager from his office who bumped into him, the substance of unknown origin that splotched his suit. He gave my father a spiteful stare, one only I caught. I laughed to myself.

You see, Tom had to accompany Aunt Cecilia, because Dad would not. He disapproved of a woman taking in the fights, of course. More than that, a matter of principle. The Newark police had a shaky relationship with boxing, he told us. Chief Long temporarily banned the sport back in 1914. When the New Jersey State Boxing Commission cited officers for an incident during a match at the First Regiment Armory in 1920, Dad swore he never again would have anything to do with it. This left Tom as the escort.

When I asked why he went, he said, "I'm still a newlywed. I'm on probation." Fair enough.

As for Orest, lately I have noticed him. Not because he is handsome, although he is. Six feet, with that strong, angular face, even if a bit asymmetrical in relationship with his neck. Those shale-blue eyes with black rings that shock at first, but remain stagnant, like an unnatural sky. He actually seemed more like the man I thought I might have married, before becoming Mrs. Morris.

No, I noticed Orest, because he almost always was at the house. After the first dinner, he returned a few nights later and then a few nights after that. He made rapid progress from guest to fixture to quasi-family member. He had come to resemble a piece of furniture that does not quite fit with the overall design, yet no one takes the time for a rearrangement, so its shape and color eventually blend with the background.

I noticed the bones that bulged in the corners of Orest's jaw when Aunt Cecilia asked him questions he did not wish to answer. And she asked many of these questions, a sort of frisky investigation that had become our entertainment most evenings.

"What's the farthest you've ever traveled?"

"What does a young fella do for fun?"

He did not respond. His silence and stillness, the perfect deflection.

I noticed something else. Aunt Cecilia and Orest could not have been more different, yet they also were quite similar. My sisters and I knew very little about either of them. Strange to say about a close family member, even if true. Orest said almost nothing, while Aunt Cecilia said too much. She poured out buckets of contradictions. Her facts and fictions mixed together so completely, you could not separate one from the other. She either had several relationships with men or none at all. She might have lived abroad or never stepped outside the city. Any person of note who ever visited Newark, she allegedly met. Or she was always on her own. My aunt had become an anecdote, one enjoyed too much by too many to disturb for the sake of honesty.

About Orest, we heard only the headlines and out-
lines. His parents, Michael and Ellen, supposedly were
two of my father's closest friends, although I cannot
recall having ever heard of them before Orest showed
up. They passed away when he was an infant. He moved
from Newark with no memory of the city. He grew up
somewhere in the southern part of the state, raised by
an aunt. He was in the army for a few years. Did not
serve overseas. He had been a police officer elsewhere
and only recently returned to Newark to join the force
in Dad's precinct. That was all. It would do. He was
more interesting the less we actually knew about him.
A mystery. When a family drops anchor in the same
city—on the same few blocks, for that matter—for a
series of generations, as ours had, you sacrifice mystery
for continuity, for history. Orest had shined a little mystery into our lives. He would have faded to normal if he
ever had answered Aunt Cecilia's questions.

A person did not require a gift or skill to notice my
father's fondness for Orest.

"Dad's son," we called him.

My father protested, but with a boyishness that
begged for more abuse.

"Stop that. What's wrong with helping him out in
the early days?"

His classification of "early days" made me wonder
if he might have understood his own joke. Historic,
if so. All foreseeable days—the early and the late—
would look like every other: Dad, on the end of the

couch, leaning athletically toward Orest, telling tales of intradepartmental politics with broad hand motions. We amused ourselves with hypothetical situations that might have distracted my father in those moments.

"House fire?"

"No."

"Earthquake?"

"Absolutely not."

"Trolley car crashing into the living room?"

"Possibly, but only if it injured Orest."

I noticed how when they talked, it seemed more like Dad delivering a monologue. Orest did not ask questions. He nodded at the appropriate points. Knew when to follow with, "Really?" and, "I've thought the same" to keep my father going. Remarkable, how effortlessly he remained as blank a canvas as possible.

More than Aunt Cecilia or my father or Catherine or Orest, himself, I noticed Amanda. This noticing required real talent, if I do say so.

I noticed her the night my father first introduced us to Orest. Tom and I arrived at the house not long after Dad and this unknown guest of his. Everyone still clogged the entryway. Before we could say anything, we heard from behind, "I was calling after you two for half-a-block. Don't tell me you didn't hear me, Tommy." Aunt Cecilia elbowed her way between us and gave Tom's ear a back-of-the-hand flick. We all crowded at the foot of the stairs and boarded a merry-go-round of hellos and hugs that eventually deposited each of us right where we had started. Amanda broke away from the group and began opening her jaw repeatedly, widely, as if trying to dislodge pressure after swimming. I pulled her into the dining room.

"What's wrong with you? You look sick."

Normally, she would have brushed me off, told me to mind my own business. Instead, she hurried to the mirror above the buffet. She yanked at her cheeks and patted down stray hairs and smoothed over her eyebrows. Not at all like her. During the meal, with the conversation gathering momentum, she stayed quiet. Ordinarily, she would have thrown at least one bolt of acerbic lightning, but no. Curious.

Even more curious, when she finally did decide to open her mouth in Orest's company.

"Where did you get that name?" Aunt Cecilia asked him rather bluntly one evening. "Couldn't have been from around here. Michael. Ellen. Those we have here. Where did you get a name like Orest?"

"Not certain," he said.

"It's short for Orestes, right?" Tom asked. "It's probably a family name. There must have been an Orestes somewhere."

"Not as far as I know."

"Well, there's Orestes Brownson, the Transcendentalist," Tom went on. "Maybe someone in your family was fond of him."

"Not sure."

"Aeschylus," Amanda said, so loudly.

"I'm sorry?" Dad asked on our behalf.

"Aeschylus, the Greek playwright. Orestes. He was one of Aeschylus' main characters."

The awkwardness climbed, fast and high. Amanda at least knew enough to not try to scale it with elaboration.

"She's right," Orest said, rescuing her, saving us all. "People have told me that."

"Amanda's our reader," Dad said, rather dismissively, eager to switch to a new topic.

Orest had spared Amanda then. Laughter would spare her a few weeks later, when she, Mom, Aunt Cecilia and I talked among ourselves after another meal, leaving the men to the living room. Rather expectedly, we turned to Orest and his filmy past, which we enjoyed making even filmier with outlandish suggestions.

"Maybe he killed someone," I said.

"I can believe it," Aunt Cecilia said. "You can see it in his eyes."

Mom offered nothing. Amanda huffed an almost-chuckle.

I then said, "Maybe he's married. Maybe his wife lives far away and doesn't even know where he is."

"No!" Amanda shouted. So big, so beyond her nature, the word should have landed as a joke at everyone's feet. My sister instead began to mold the laughable into the logical. "He couldn't be, when you think about it. Dad would know, right? Right?"

Before any of us could answer her—and by "answer," I really mean question—Aunt Cecilia said, "Well, maybe he killed his wife."

The four of us laughed, loud and hard. So loud and so hard, Amanda's pseudo-admission snuck away undetected, unremembered below the noise. No one else noticed. But I did. And from that point, I continued to notice.

CHAPTER FOUR

Catherine

I wanted to play baseball with Orest.

A game of catch. Maybe have him pitch to me, so I could show him how far I could hit. I was better than most of the boys in the neighborhood. You wouldn't believe it unless you could see it. I wanted Orest to see. I wasn't as interesting as Elizabeth. Not as smart as Amanda. Baseball would get his attention.

"Do you like baseball?" I asked him.

"I do. I've played a little."

"Great. First nice day, we'll play together?"

"Deal."

I had his attention.

Because I would come home so filthy after being outside, Mom didn't like how much I enjoyed playing. But Dad did. Maybe because he didn't have a son. Maybe because Amanda and Elizabeth never showed any interest. And, yes, maybe I told him I liked baseball, even though I didn't at first, so the two of us could have something to do together. A third daughter doesn't get to do much the first two already haven't done.

Dad took me to Bears' games. The stands and crowds bothered me at first. The long, boring quiet, then the stomping and shouting. The game grew on me. The world seemed so big and open inside Harrison Park. I thought the rest of the country must look the same, especially out West. So big and open and green and breezy. When Dad would tell me to keep my eye on a player, it felt like a secret he shared only with me. Not with my sisters or my mother. Only me.

"Baldwin's got the stuff. He'll get called up."

"Brainard's near the end, but he still has something left. He wasn't bad in his day."

Last year, Dad thought the Bears would have a decent showing. They finished fifty-four and one-hundred-and-twelve.

"This season," he said at the end of the last game, "deserves forgetting."

I didn't care if they won or lost. I still looked forward to Opening Day. And maybe I was worried with Orest around, Dad wouldn't need me to go with him. I had to prove I belonged. I wanted to be the one to walk Orest around Harrison Park, to point out where we usually sat, to talk about the shallow and deep parts of the outfield. I wanted to show him I knew how to keep score, how I would stay until the very end of every game, even with extra innings. I tried to bring baseball up during our meals.

"Did you know they're building a new stadium in New York, for the Yankees? Right, Dad?"

"She's right."

"That would be my dream, to go to a game when it opens."

"Dream big," Elizabeth said. I knew she was putting me down.

"I like that dream," Orest said, coming to my defense.

Sometimes, when I would head to bed before everyone or when Orest would leave the house, I would remind him, "First nice day, we'll play, right?"

"Right," he said.

This started in November, so we probably couldn't play until April. Maybe the end of March, because it can warm up on some days. I've also seen it snow in April, so no guarantees. I would have to wait.

Until that day in December.

So hot and sunny. In the high fifties, the day felt like the warmest of the year, probably because we expected the cold. Everyone had something to say about it, too. Teachers. My friends. Their parents.

"Is it really December?"

"Can you get your head around this heat?"

"Polar bears must be sweating."

I didn't care what people thought about the weather. I only cared about one thing: *Today's the day*. I didn't listen very well during class. Just looked out the window. One of the nuns scolded me. ("Miss Bannon, are we keeping you from something?") When the sun went behind the clouds and the sky darkened for a minute, my heart slid down into my stomach. I was losing. The sun broke through, more brightly than before.

School over, I ran home. Would have to grab my glove and find Orest. I might've had to go to the precinct and listen politely to the other officers say, "Look who's all grown up!" and, "Who's this lady? Can't be Catherine." I wouldn't have the time. Or patience. The day might've felt like spring, but the sun still would set early. I was so anxious. But when I got to the house, Orest was sitting on the front stoop, with his glove and ball.

"You promised," he said. "First nice day."

Relief and warmth and happiness, all at once, all through me. I almost cried.

Along the sidewalks, coats thrown down by all of the children, our mothers having demanded we take them. They thought winter might wake up, look at the calendar and hit us with a blizzard to make up for the sunshine. Across Pennsylvania Avenue, tagging and jumping. Everyone playing games with no rules. Orest and I were in the center of the street. He still wore his uniform. No one would give us much of a problem.

At first, he stood too close to me. He didn't think I could throw very far.

"Keep going," I shouted as he walked backward.

"Are you sure?"

"Keep going."

He looked surprised when the ball reached him with a sharp pop sound as it hit his glove.

"You weren't kidding," he said. "You are good."

After a few back-and-forth tosses, I could tell he wasn't throwing as hard as he could.

"You can throw harder," I said. "I can handle it."

He wouldn't throw harder. I had to show him. I stretched my right shoulder as far back as I could without falling down, then whipped my arm like a catapult. The ball sailed high over Orest's head. Beyond his range, I thought. I assumed he would've let it fall behind him, then walk to pick it up or wait for one of the neighborhood children to send it over. He would say, "Sorry, Catherine. I'll throw for real."

But no.

He didn't sprint as much as glide, back and farther back, clearing house after house without any effort. Without even looking, the ball sank into his glove. Impressive. In one motion, he bounced on his right leg and spun three-hundred-and-sixty degrees, releasing to me at the perfect point in his rotation. The full turn completed, he faced away from me, his hands on his knees.

"Whoa!" I said. "I've never seen one of the Bears do that."

Right beyond Orest, I saw Amanda. I don't know when she started watching us. She must've seen the catch and the throw, because she smiled. And I didn't see her smile very often. No one did.

CHAPTER FIVE

Margaret

I only could do the waiting.

As usual.

Had done so much waiting in my life, I might have thought I had perfected it. This, though, was a different type of waiting. I wanted it to end, yes, as one almost always does. I also wanted to wait endlessly, to stay in that state. What would follow, I could not conceive.

I had tried to keep myself busy since the early afternoon, since we had returned to the house. Nothing worked. Nothing could distract me. I only could do the waiting. Waited in the kitchen, not the living room or dining room. The living room or dining room would have felt like relaxation. And this was not relaxation. The kitchen at least felt like work, even if I could not bring myself to do anything.

Waiting to give bad news might be worse than waiting to receive bad news. I would have suspected the opposite before this day. He really had no idea what was to come. I envied him and resented him at once, as I often did. To be so free of such news, even for a few minutes more, such a gift. To be oblivious to such news, almost a sin.

In late February, everything becomes so dark so early. Had to check the clock, because three in the afternoon can look like midnight. And it was after five, so I expected him. But I did not expect him to shout my name when he walked through the front door.

"Margaret! Margaret!"

In reply, he heard nothing. I could not give him the reaction he wanted. Not on this night. Maybe never again. Excitement always seemed to impair Joseph's senses. Odd, since senses, he had bragged, were the tools of his vocation. He did not see how the living-room lamps were out. He did not hear the astonishing quiet. He did not take note of how no aroma came from the kitchen. He did not feel the calm and dread. Finally showed myself, all puffy eyes and porridge skin, hunched and hollow, feet dragging on the floor. None of this registered with him. He only saw an audience eager to hear his news.

"Margaret, you should've heard what they said about him today. Sergeant. They want to make him a sergeant. Before the end of the year. Can you believe it?"

My husband, weeks ago, had dispensed with Orest's name. He relied on personal pronouns. Only one "he" or "him" lived in his world.

"Came here in October and they already want to move him up. No one has done it so fast. No one."

I winced, his volume so out of touch. Thought my stare could rouse some self-awareness, but no.

"He won't be able to come over tonight, but I want to celebrate, even if it—"

"Joseph."

"We should do something soon, right? I'd like to have everyone here. Maybe one or two of the others from the precinct. Maybe not. Not until it's official. I wouldn't want to ruin—"

"We saw Doctor Caputo today."

The name ripped the phonograph needle off his spinning moment. The room screeched still. A sleepwalker jerked awake, he took stock of his surroundings. Dim and cold and noiseless. Might have resembled any number of the crime scenes he had walked into over the years. What historically followed "Caputo" robbed my husband of those best-case scenarios that had let him sleep at night. (Him, not me.) He went to sit in an armchair, then switched to the couch, for no reason other than delay. He first focused on the meaningless.

"Why? Why today? Why didn't you tell me? I should've been there."

"She hasn't been feeling well since Christmas, probably before then. She's been tired. More headaches. She didn't want to worry any of us. She collapsed at work today."

"I should've been there." So stubborn, so insignificant.

"It happened quickly. Saint Barnabas sent someone to the house. I didn't think it was anything terrible. Maybe the flu or maybe she hadn't eaten enough. She hasn't been eating much lately. They started these tests, new ones they'd never done before. And they kept going, so there wasn't time to stop and find you. I thought we would be back here in the afternoon, that we would be telling you about it together. The same as always. More rest. Some pills. Something. Not this."

I tried to recall as many details as possible from Doctor Caputo's office, because Joseph would start to ask questions and I hoped to stop him before he began. I was too sad to also feel stupid. "Her white cell count is high, the highest it's ever been." Thought numbers might do it. Thought enough numbers might add up in his head, so I would not have to finish the math for him. Did not work. He sat there, waiting for more.

"Less than a year. Doctor Caputo said she has less than a year."

"He's a liar." My husband shot from his seat, stomping in a mad circle, as if the news could be collared and thrown in a cell, like one of his criminals. "He's a liar. We'll find another doctor, one who knows what the hell he's doing."

I typically would have considered his responses in advance. Would have walked myself through the scenarios. *If he says 'this,' I will do 'that.' If he brings up 'this,' I will remind him of 'that.'* Spent more energy on making him feel better than I ever did on managing my own feelings. Not then. I was annihilated. Only habit continued to beat my heart and pump my lungs.

"We've been to them."

"I'm not willing to give up now."

There it was. Whom did he indict? Who was giving up? Doctor Caputo or me? His glare flooded the room, yet still preserved a cowardly I-did-not-mean-you island for retreat. But he did mean me. Or he did not. I could not decide. I did not want to know, really. Some people—the uninitiated or the dense—believe one answer to a single question makes a union. ("Will you marry me?" "Yes.") So very wrong, I had learned. Millions upon millions of answers pound a marriage into scraps and glue it back together. Unless and until the adhesives of patience and compromise and acceptance run dry. Mine had run dry at that very moment. Years logged can twist love into nothing more than the limitless accommodation of the other. ("He's under stress." "He doesn't mean it." "That's not what he intended.") How many accommodations until one discovers a limit, in fact, exists? Might require a transcendent insensitivity. Might require an instance like right then. The rusted, loose rivets of our bond stripped down.

In those seconds, I held together the walls, the ceiling, the floor, our marriage with my severe squint. Blink and it all would have flown away in different directions. Tried to see the person who had proposed to me with a sweet stammer. The narrow frame of my view, cloudy at the edges, cropped his middle-age jowls, the slight column of a younger, gentler man visible enough to remind me why I cared for him at all, why I had not fled right then or the hundreds of occasions before this night. I detested him at times. He probably never knew. Detested how I could not state mild displeasure without knocking down the fragile beams that propped up his universe.

Would it have been this way with the others? I projected onto sag-sitting Joseph the fuzzy images of those attentive men from years fewer and fewer people seemed to remember. Boys, uncorrupted by age and everyday negotiation, looking better in fantasy than ever in reality. Charles. George. All of them. They made promises, too. Promises of adoration and fun. Would theirs have kept better than his? No, but maybe yes. Maybe. If nothing else, my life would have been changed, perhaps only slightly. Slightly, though, matters. Slightly separates daughters from illness. Genes and cells would have mixed and merged in a way that would have pardoned Amanda, pardoned me. Such a tempting vision. If only I could have abandoned the present for the past. If only I could. The future, too. Gladly would have surrendered the future in the exchange.

"I'm sorry," he said, so ignorant of how he might have salvaged our marriage. "What do we do?"

There he was. I was back with him, almost disappointed at the lost escape. He traded his vulnerability so recklessly for my strength, always expecting to receive it. The expectation tightened the veins around my throat, shoved my tongue hard against the back of my teeth.

"We've done everything," I said, assuring myself as much as him. "We knew this would come. We got away before. Not now. The doctors told us. I wanted to think we could, even if she didn't. She knew. She always knew. She's smart. Too smart. Only a matter of time. There never was going to be enough of it."

"Not as much of it as we deserved," he said.

My mouth moved as if I prepared to say something. A rebuke? A lament? Only a motion, an impulse. I did not know what word I might have chosen. I would have had to invent one to capture his impossible self-centeredness, the sadness, the cruelty, the loss. Instead, a thick pause in which I again wished I could say to him: "I do not want to be around you. Not now. Not ever." Suppose he would tell me the same, if he ever could step off the stage of our passive-aggressive theater.

The last fragments of daylight had left through the curtain slits hours earlier. Wished I could have tagged along with them to wherever they traveled next, perhaps to a part of the planet without sick daughters and thoughtless husbands. Joseph sat in his chair, weighed down, I suspect, by one word: *should*. He *should* comfort me. He *should* feel a certain way. He *should* meet the occasion with strength, as if he even knew what that meant. He did none of them. One *should* he could not avoid. I would not let him.

"I should go see her," he said weakly, a question mark almost strolling in at the end.

"She's in her room."

He waited another minute, as if each new tick of the second hand somehow could save him. Lurched left-to-right to pull himself up. At the bottom stair, he touched the bannister and paused. He likely remembered how he had tried not to engage Amanda on ordinary days. She knew him too well. She persecuted him with upturned eyes of annoyance and pity. The annoyance he probably could take. Parents accept it as unfortunate collateral. Her pity and its know-it-all, poor-man condescension, that pushed him a little farther away from her each time.

"College? Why?" he had said when she shared what she would like to do after graduating from Saint Vincent's. Joseph congratulated himself for the eventual compromise of a small job first, with enrollment in a university in the fall of 1923. Marked a signature victory in his role as her father, the one to which he always pointed to convince himself he had done right by her, despite all else. Parenthood had become negotiation to him, at least with Amanda.

I watched him trudge up the staircase. He delayed outside her bedroom door for a few gutless moments. He probably hoped Catherine would show up. So much easier to be one of three than of two. He would have consoled his youngest daughter. Amanda would have swooped in with some optimistic sentiment. Father and middle daughter would have connected through Catherine. Would have let him believe he had done enough. He would not be so lucky. No rescue by Catherine.

Finally, I heard the knocks, light and fast.

CHAPTER SIX

Amanda

"Come in," I said.

The door creaked open and there stood my father, apprehensive over what he might discover. Hysteria. Hostility. Catatonia. Strange, how he had raised daughters for over two decades, yet we still seemed so alien to him. Dad saw a picture possibly taken on any one of a thousand nights: I sat in the windowsill. How many more chances to find me there? Twenty? Ten?

No words from him, only breath through the small, cracked-whistle opening of his lips. A broken toy, the wind-up gear in his back having malfunctioned, stranding him in the doorway, shoulders stooped. He had brought himself that far. I would have to do the rest. I left the ledge and sat on the end of the bed. Patted an invitation for him to join me. He did.

"Told your mother we should see more doctors," he said, so predictably deaf. "I'm not ready to give up. They must be doing something somewhere—"

"Dad," I stopped him, my hand on his wrist, applying a degree of pressure between affection and aggression. I could not listen to another explanation of what was best, a nauseating trip back to those fit-filled discussions from childhood. Among my first recollections: the anger of wanting to know more. Men in coats poked my tiny body with frozen instruments in rooms scrubbed with chemicals. They scribbled on paper, then whispered to Mom and Dad phrases I could not understand.

"What did they say?" I asked through tears. "What did they say?"

My parents told me nothing, only throwaway lines. "Just adult talk." "Not much to worry about." I knew enough to worry. First, brooding tantrums and days-long fasts. Around eleven, I went to books. At least one-third of the medical publications in Newark, I believe I had read. A short-burst hobby, Mom and Dad assumed at first. Something picked up and soon discarded. Not quite. I sustained an hours-upon-hours tenacity that familiarized me with human physiology, with words like "hemoglobin" and "lymphatic" in my speech. By thirteen or fourteen, I had mastered more than many of the professionals who examined me. I would sling at them questions about treatments and research they would bobble and lateral to experts conveniently unavailable. Their rolled-eye exasperation, itself a reward.

I irritated most of them, but not Doctor Caputo. Confident and unconventional, with two daughters of his own, he spotted talent. He arranged for my job at

Saint Barnabas after high school. Told me about Woman's Medical College in Philadelphia. From fifteen, my plan: work at the hospital, off to college, then to Pennsylvania for medical school to become Doctor Bannon.

By January, my condition began to read like the worst passages I had studied. I never indulged in hypochondria. No, I took notes each day, tracking my decline, measurement by measurement. Science. Empiricism. I kept not my records, but those of a faceless patient. Even still, every jot in the pad rewrote my history. College ... erased. Philadelphia ... erased. Any type of career ... erased.

Doctor Caputo handed down his final diagnosis with a splash of emotion that soddened the ground between the personal and professional, a puddle into which I refused to step. Confirmation. Only wanted confirmation. Knew my work—all of it—would lead to one of two moments: graduation from medical school or that one, when I would accept the outcome. I had invested too much for sentimentality. Instead, I posed to Doctor Caputo questions about timing and phases and palliative methods. What good would the reading have been otherwise? What good? What was the point of study if not acceptance? That Dad tried to take from me this acceptance lit a fuse. He grasped not a fraction of what I had earned, yet he insisted on possessing trite insight. Not even insight. A form of control costumed as paternal tenderness. Such damage I could have done with what I might have said next. Could have ended of our relationship, several months ahead of schedule. Instead, a calm came over me. I raised my left eyebrow and shook my head.

Even Dad understood. He retreated with a look to the floor and said, "I'm just sorry."

He held my hand, helplessness in his flexed-forearm veins. Smacked the base of his left palm to the bridge of his nose, massaged his eye socket and breathed heavily.

"You got a bad deal," he said, rapping his fist against my knee. "About the worst around. Anything you want, Amanda."

"Nothing, thank you."

"Wasn't a question. Anything you want. You get anything you want."

"Excuse me?"

"Listen, say I don't understand or that I'm short-sighted or whatever, but take this seriously. Anything you want," he repeated with confidence, "and it's yours. I mean it. Let me do this for you. Europe? Do you want to go to Europe? We'll figure out a way to get you there."

I felt sorry for him. He could resort only to the transactional. All he knew to do, all he ever would know to do, if at his age and at that instant he could satisfy himself only with such a gesture.

"Europe? What's this about?"

"I have to be able to do something," he said, an admission of self-interest that disarmed me. "Anything you want, Amanda. Anything in the world."

"I don't know. Have to think about it."

"Do that," he told me, as if delivering orders to his officers. That type of control, however illusory, fell naturally into his grip.

"Right now," I dropped my neck, "I need some rest."

I pulled up my legs into my chest, fell to my side and straightened out flat on my back. Dad covered me with the blanket from the foot of the bed. He could have kissed my head and said, "I love you, Amanda." He did not.

I turned over, facing the window. In a few seconds, the idea came to me. From where, I did not know. Likely from the subconscious kettle of motivation in which the absurd, the outrageous and the egotistical so often stir together. If ever I would tip over that kettle and let the contents spill out, had to be then. No time for assessment. I had all of the figures right where I wanted them, if I ever wanted them anywhere at all. Postponing the conversation with my father, even for a few minutes, could have weakened my position.

If I had said later that same night, "Dad, when you said I could have anything—"

"Anything within reason, Amanda," he could have answered, already tapering his terms.

Could have ended it.

Unable to see him, I could feel his eyes on me, still filmed by regret. I needed every molecule of that regret. For such an immense proposition, I would have to lean on every hideously manipulative advantage. Out the bedroom with him would go those advantages. Before he could reach the door, I called out, the sound low, one ear pressed to the pillow, a whir in my head.

"Dad, there might be something I want."

CHAPTER SEVEN

The Aunt

At the breakfast table especially, I did not know when to speak or when to stay silent. I never could judge his appetite for engagement. Not there, in the dining room. Nor in the bedroom. In the mornings, he held his head at an angle at which his eyes could take in or ignore everything before him: his plate, his middle-folded newspaper, me. Had he patented that angle? Had he worked on it over the years, trying out different gradations? Did an etiquette instructor teach him? Or was it natural, something passed on from each successive generation of uninterested men?

During meals, when I would introduce a topic, he would bark, "I'm reading." If I were too quiet, he would ask, "Is there nothing on your mind?" Such a nervous way to live. That morning, his pauses, so cavernous, so frosty, I worried I would fall into them and stay there forever. Maybe not so unwelcome. A place to hide in peace.

"I never wanted one," he said, still scanning the headlines.

"I know." I often felt like the disciplined child of a disappointed parent. "I didn't either."

"Then why have you brought one into my home?" That slit stare of his always caged me.

"I didn't have much of a choice."

"I disagree." He snapped the newspaper up in a dramatic whoosh, holding it in front of him, hiding his entire self. "I thought you hated your brother."

"I do." Hate felt wrong and cruel after what had happened. "I did. More apathy than hate."

To call it apathy felt like a lie. Closer to hate. "Was it worth it?" The last words my brother had spoken to me five years earlier. Maybe my memory had tricked me, led me to believe he had said something more poetic and violent, like, "I have no sister." How I remembered it, what I kept with me all of the days since. Perhaps I needed poetry and violence to stay away. We sometimes have to transform the mundane into the villainous. The blast of the news blew off the dirt. Clean and clear, the scene came back to me. "Was it worth it?" That was what he had said.

The business meetings in Manhattan had brought me home then. Two overnights in the city, my husband in boardrooms all day. I had enough time on my own for a trip across the river. The streets and houses in the neighborhood had changed so little. Brown and gray columns, different heights, different widths. Smudged windows and chipped stoops. My home definitely seemed to have shrunk. Such a prison. Such a cave. I stood on the sidewalk across the street, stretched out my arm and held up my hand, my palm covering the house. I laughed. I finally felt bigger than all of it. I felt bigger than everything that had occurred inside.

At the front door, no one answered. I waited and knocked, waited and knocked. Moved around to the side, propping up on my toes, trying to see into the kitchen window. A suspicious neighbor eyed me. Not Mrs. Flannery. She must have relocated. Maybe died. Someone new. Nothing to explain to this woman. I decided to take a walk, down to the park, over by the school, all around the maze of my youth, the distant scent of hops from the Hensler Brewery in the air. Not one person recognized me. An older man I passed smiled, but only out of hospitality. Had I really shed the place so completely? No native trace in my style, in my bearing? That alone, a victory.

Back at the house, I sat on the front steps, like when a little girl waiting for my father. Even after he had died, when I was ten, I still would sit, waiting for him, hoping he might reappear. Only a few more minutes before I had to return to Manhattan. I did not plan to write a note. Someone surely would tell them I had visited. A man in uniform rounded the far corner. I knew his walk, how his swaying shoulders powered his legs. Not so much his frame, which had thickened up all over. A middle-aged woman from across the street ran out to meet him. She pointed in my direction. His eyes followed. I had no idea if he recognized me. I had grown older myself. He did not say a word to the neighbor, abandoning her on the sidewalk, motioning and talking after him.

When he reached the front walkway, I stood and tried to smile. I had not come to fight, but then again, I really did not know why I had come. I should have thought of an answer, because he probably would have asked. He did not. He stepped past me without a sound.

"Hello," I said.

Nothing. Just the jangle of his keys.

"Where's Mom?"

My brother paused, rubbed the outside corners of his eyes with his thumb and index finger. He said as he opened the door, "She passed away about ten months ago."

"She's dead?" I followed him inside. "Why didn't you tell me?"

He stopped in the entryway. His stance, with his legs shoulder-width apart, commanded I go no farther.

"I should've been at her funeral," I said.

"She should've been at your wedding," he snapped, a coil waiting years to spring.

"It's about my marriage?"

He gave me that twisted-dimple smirk of his, which I could have done without seeing ever again. "We assumed Catholics couldn't go to Protestant weddings. Same for Protestants at Catholic funerals."

"That's wrong."

"Wrong, maybe. Also, the truth."

"Really? You're going to be smug after keeping me from my dying mother?"

"I didn't. She did. If she had wanted to see you, we would've found you. But she didn't."

I gagged, as if the words had broken down into individual letters in my mouth. I could have spat out an "H" or an "L," but not a word, let alone a sentence. A beaten expression drizzled onto my face. I spun, my back to him. I gathered myself for about ten seconds. I swiveled around, fearsomely so. Immovable, he gave me no chance to get beyond him. I swiped a fast look over his shoulder: the den, the corner of the dining room, the kitchen. So different from the picture in my mind.

"Should never have come back here," I said.

"There we agree."

I gripped the front doorknob, so slippery and loose, unable to slide into its groove. Always had given me trouble.

"Was it worth it?" my brother asked.

"He's crying."

"What?" Back with my husband, back in the moment.

"The child. He's crying upstairs," he pointed out from behind the paper. "Aren't you going to do something about it?"

"One of the girls will get him."

Ruination. The ruination of family lies in the endless debate over who did worse to whom. Pain and aggression deposit rubble, leaving so little to rebuild.

"I really don't think this will change much," I started with a manufactured pertness. "We have enough help.

The girls can manage. He'll be in school before we know it. We'll send him away somewhere, like up to New England. You won't even notice him. By the time we get back from California—"

The newspaper down. "California?" my husband repeated. "I don't think you should go. It's for business."

"I've gone on business trips before."

"Things have changed. You have responsibilities now." He raised the paper. Point made. No discussion. "I can still hear him."

"What?"

"I can still hear the baby. They don't know what they're doing. Go up and see."

I obeyed. Left the table, left him to his breakfast, off to the second floor.

Was it worth it?

CHAPTER EIGHT

Amanda

"It's too short," Mom told me.

"That's the style," said Elizabeth. "It's not much shorter than mine was."

"If she likes it, let her get it," Aunt Cecilia added. "Suits her."

The comments swirled around me, rubbish in an alley, lifted and spun by a hard breeze. So much speculation since Orest had agreed to marry me. Up on the hollow, wooden, half-foot pedestal in the Hahne's women's department, scrutiny pinched and bruised my body, opinions about dresses allowing for criticism too sharp to voice and too long suppressed.

My wedding would take place on the first Saturday in March at Saint Columba's. Father Scanlon had agreed to marry us in the church, despite the pretense. I recognized how I had stranded my family in emotional limbo. Thought they might be grateful, getting to plan a wedding instead of a funeral. But no, not grateful. Just confused. I saw the confusion in their bloodshot expressions, their scramble for words. This confusion, I enjoyed.

First, my father. Dad met my request to marry Orest with a broad smile, believing it a joke. Reality then set in and his grin flattened into a stern, horizontal plank. I had veered so wildly from his sense of me. There were Aunt Cecilia and Elizabeth. With their blithe-sad expressions, they viewed me as a combination of disease, marvel, secrecy and tragedy. No longer the pathetic, sick sister-niece. I liked how I had shocked them. My family members perhaps had sketched out my final scenes: a few poignant lines, my appreciative response, then gone. No, I took it from them, happily so.

Is that why I did it?

Maybe. Maybe not.

Regardless, the confusion, I enjoyed.

Until I did not.

All they would not say had made everything too uncomfortable. Walking around the halls, down the stairs, we bumped into one another, as if blindfolded and left to feel our way around a rush-hour train station. "Excuse me," they said. *I wish I had stayed in my room*, I read in their faces. In those moments, it seemed as if the thin rifts around the doors and window frames had sealed shut, the internal pressure building and building so intolerably high. I feared an explosion would collapse the foundation of One-Hundred-Twelve Pennsylvania Avenue, our home splitting in half, all of us caked in plaster, concrete and glass.

Out of necessity, I offered a release.

"We should shop for my wedding dress," I said to my mother one morning.

"Your wedding dress," she repeated. The news registered first in her right hand. Her fingers uncoiled slowly, stretching out fully, her palm open as wide as possible. Then my other family members exhaled, as did the house, itself, the walls and floorboards croaking and expanding in relief. The following day, my nose stuffed with fabric dye and sample perfume, my ears whizzing with the tinny, fast scrapes of hangers across racks, I stood like a sacrifice on an altar of contrivance.

"Try this one," Aunt Cecilia called from across the store, shoppers' heads turning in her direction.

"You really should wear something that accentuates your positive features," Elizabeth said.

Positive features? Where? All lost in the prodding and pulling, the frowns, the whispers, the snobby euphemisms. ("That doesn't really show you off well.") Too many opinions to consider. Finally, in the mirror, an image only vaguely conceived: a cream-colored dress both elegant and subtle. Exhaustion or satisfaction convinced me this was the one. Did it matter? I needed the search to end. Closed-lidded and tight-lipped, I would not change into another suggestion. Mom motioned her surrender, calling over the salesperson to complete the purchase.

"We did it," Elizabeth said.

"We did," Aunt Cecilia agreed, the two taking me in with some vain notion of accomplishment.

"I think she looks terrible," a sick-and-tired voice intruded on the self-congratulation.

"Catherine!" Mom said.

"Take it back," Elizabeth said.

"No, don't take it back. Tell me," I wanted to say to Catherine, with her sneering, teenage hardheaded-ness. I admired her unwillingness to withdraw under oops-I'm-sorry cover. She meant it. She meant so much more, her mouth crumpling in twitchy spasms, ready to spit out some scalding compound of hormones, grief and jealousy. I wanted her anger, to hear a person call me stupid and thoughtless. I wanted the truth, not another aesthetic critique. Only Catherine had the courage and immaturity to tell me, however distorted by her moony captivation with Orest. Before she again could speak, Mom ordered her away with Elizabeth and Aunt Cecilia.

"She's having a hard time with it," my mother said as we waited for the dress.

"It" never before had sounded so ambiguous. I paused in my head on the word "ambiguous," the "big" shimmering with the boldfaced glow of the Loew's marquee on Broad Street. This was big for Catherine: losing her sister to an illness she could not comprehend, while having that same sister spoil her puppy-love infatuation. Such a betrayal. If not for my wedding, Mom and Dad would have avoided a terrible conversation with Catherine and her all-too-legitimate question: "Why?" Why was her sister dying? Why was

she marrying Orest? With either, my parents probably mopped up the mess with quaint fatalism: "Just
because." The unanswerable. We each eventually have
to deal with the unanswerable. Catherine likely began
to deal with it right then, thanks to me. Resistance and
rage. Denial and happiness. Acceptance and peace.
Maybe. Maybe not, for her. She would become the
one always seeking or the one always sought.

"It" was big for Catherine. "It" was big for all of us.

Except for Orest, at least from appearance.

"He'll do it," my father said, standing in my bedroom doorway only hours after I had given my answer
to his "Anything you want" offer. He had gone to see
Orest at Mrs. Sullivan's boarding house that same night.
Some combination of disgust and relief rinsed around
his mouth as he delivered the news.

"Really?" A second-thought cannonball rammed
right through my midsection, the hole opening wider
and wider.

Dad closed the door before I could pelt him with
questions: What was Orest's mood? Angry? Sympathetic? What had he said? The next morning, I
remained in bed too long, wondering how my father
had done it. Such an unconventional proposal. What
terms had he set? What argument did he use? Any
threats? Any rewards? I did not want to know. None
of it mattered.

But some of it did. Orest mattered. His deliberation. His motivation. His misgivings. All could mix

together and poison to death his generosity. Or perhaps not. I had no true understanding of him, this man who would become my husband. I was certain only that I could have saved each of us aggravation by holding back a few sentences. Those so-close alternatives throbbed in my neck, up through my jaw. I turned over, pillow against the back of my head, my face raking side-to-side in the mattress, taunted by the image of a different day. A day in which I would have had to manage nothing more than the aftermath of Doctor Caputo's diagnosis.

Instead, I would eat that evening at the same table with my fiancé, if the term even applied to someone lured into marriage by the desperate father of a dying girl. What would be more appropriate? *Phon*-iancé? *Fraud*-iancé? *Arti*-fiancé? Amusing, but a delay tactic. Mental chewing gum, really, to keep my mind from the embarrassment of facing him. I had no plan, as if I had jumped off a cliff and were surprised to learn I would continue falling.

I was curious. Anxious, yes. Mortified, yes. But mostly curious. I might have locked myself in my bedroom until the day of the wedding, but I had to see his immediate response. Again, almost like a science experiment. Would Orest be even quieter? Perhaps more relaxed and engaging, the marriage having activated dormant personality traits? Whether I wished to or not, I soon would discover during dinner. I made my way downstairs and stayed inside the dining room, arranging forks and spoons. I circled and circled the table, pretending each and every utensil engrossed me.

Orest arrived. I committed more ferociously to the task, picking up knives and rubbing out phantom water spots. My family members puddled around him, hoping he could sober them up with light and heat. To an extent, he did. He was normal. Greeted them as he had on any other occasion, without mention of my health or the wedding. His normality, a dose of counterintuitive medicine. He visited from an unaffected world, one that rotated without interruption, one that awaited them when the events—and I—had passed.

I entered.

"Amanda."

All Orest said. Not even "Hello, Amanda." Only "Amanda." His demeanor would not change, not for death, not for marriage. Reassuring, I suppose, especially during the first dinner. His consistency calmed us. By the second dinner, though, it bothered me. The unreferenced wedding sat like a massive, powder-keg centerpiece. Aunt Cecilia holstered her smart-aleck cap guns. Tom introduced no trivia. Catherine said nothing about baseball. Finally, midway through an agonizing third meal, Mom said, "We thought two-thirty for the ceremony."

"That works," Orest said, direct and detached, with a clear sub-message: *All I will say about that.* His answer, enough for the rest of the family, enough for them to return to their meals and resume their lives. Not for me. A that's-it disbelief scrunched my nose, my top teeth exposed. I gave him a now-or-never stare. Expected to sponge up his judgment, then wring it down my throat, into my stomach, fuel for an antagonistic, I'll-show-you march down the aisle.

But he gave me nothing. Not a flinch. Not a nod. Just a void where I could rummage for recognition, likely never to find any. Irony. I might have found irony. Again to Sister Mary Rose and her almost ruthless indoctrination not to confuse "irony" and "coincidence," with those who misspoke having to write fifty times the following: "Words or situations that differ from or oppose the intended or the expected." I hesitated to hint at irony, my knuckle aching at the memory of secondary-school penalties. But this might have been ironic. A plan designed to bring us closer together set us farther apart. Was it even a plan? That question could flatten out the convolutions of my brain into a parchment inscribed with insanity.

Cancel. I would cancel the wedding, I had resolved at least ten times each night, flopping on sheets matted with sweat and worry. Or die. Die before the wedding. Die and avoid it all. Could happen. So much easier that way. My family would mourn me as intended, whisking up the marriage nonsense into the canister that hid secrets and mistakes.

But no.

The wedding had to come across either as expertly planned or wholly arbitrary. In-between would cast me a fool. So much better to be capricious or calculating than a fool. If I had called it off, Elizabeth surely would have come to my door with eyebrows raised, her head at a perfectly patronizing angle, the poor-thing, I-told-you-so conclusion to whatever conversations had taken place behind my back. Would not do. I would go through with the wedding to wipe that expression off her face. Obstinacy carried me, as always. Marriages had proceeded on less pragmatic grounds, I reasoned.

On the morning of Elizabeth's wedding, I remember the arms of the chairs in the living room blinded with a wet, dark-walnut shine. The curtains flapped in a breeze of freesia and cake icing. Mom presided over a squadron of helpers. The bride-to-be walked around in calligraphic motions. Dad focused on any detail to deaden the sadness of giving away his first daughter. Such a delightfully unnecessary extravaganza.

On the morning my wedding, I breathed in a muggy inertia, the house filled with slept-in-bed-linen air. The downstairs curtains remained drawn, curious on any day, but damning on this one. My family might have wished to hide the scene from the public. Over breakfast, my parents acted like bashful children, ostrich heads jammed down into meals. I counted the day from that point forward, first in hours, then in minutes. At least I could reduce the experience to something calculable. When I excused myself from the table, Mom asked, "When would you like us ready?"

"Two, I suppose," I said. The question seemed odd, without a definite sense as to why, the sentence staying with me as I prepared myself. *When would you like us ready? When would you like us ready?* I fixed my own hair and applied my own makeup. Not like Elizabeth's wedding. Two people for this. Three for that. *There!* In the contrast, the discovery. *When would you like us ready?* Mom never would have asked such a question of my sister. Her wedding, a cooperative. Everyone owned a share of the event. Not mine. I possessed my day entirely and exclusively. A prideful bicep bulge in my right arm with the few final brush strokes.

At two o'clock, as requested, my family gathered near the front door. They looked like marbles in a sack: matte-colored, sheened, hard and anxious over impact. I walked down the stairs, steady and confident. As my foot shook in the drop between the last step and the floor, Elizabeth said, "I told you this dress was the one."

"We should go," I said, cutting off any further comments.

March suited my wedding. Out the door, we made our way down Pennsylvania Avenue under a colorless sky that ached for daylight. No words among us. Only the crunch of shoe leather and the wisp-wisp rustle of coats sounded among us. Block-by-block, we broke gradually into a floating archipelago, the men to the rear, Mom and Catherine hanging in the middle. I was out in front with Elizabeth and Aunt Cecilia.

Once inside Saint Columba's, Father Scanlon's friendly "There you are" boomed like a brass instrument through the arches. For hundreds and hundreds of minutes, we had listened to his sick-mallard, sing-song voice, inhaled the same incense, stared at the back of his white-haired, ruddy skull during mass.

"This will be a little different from Elizabeth and Tom's," he began, leading us down the aisle, jousting with Aunt Cecilia: "They let you attend, I see." Near the first few pews, he stopped mid-sentence. Turned around and asked, "Someone missing?"

"What did Orest tell you yesterday?" Mom asked Dad.

"I didn't see him."

"You didn't confirm?"

Below their bickering, a he-might-not-show apprehension. The slow groan of the opening door saved us from a worst-case scenario.

"There," Dad said with the zing of exoneration.

The stained glass filtered an afternoon dusk that made Orest a scarcely discernible shadow drifting toward us. I noticed the hesitancy, the weight of our attention pulling his heels into the maroon carpet. If he could have foreseen this procession, he surely would have declined. Too much for his nature. My nature normally would have advised I slip into the pack of Bannons, into the shelter of semi-anonymity. But no. Not on this day. I broke from the others and moved toward him. Dad leaned to follow me, but Mom hooked him by the elbow. At the center of Saint Columba's—almost parallel to the sixth Station of the Cross—we met.

"Orest."

"Amanda."

When he spoke my name, I returned not to the initial dinner after our unusual engagement. No, I returned to October, when I first saw him. The two moments were not related, of course. I could not help but feel this second moment somehow fulfilled the first, maybe willed into effect by me or perhaps something beyond me.

"Shall we?" I said.

Orest slowly dipped his chin down toward his right shoulder, taking me in through his left eye.

"I've got nowhere else to be," he said with a slight smirk.

By the altar, the group divided into males and females. On one side, I overheard Tom express feigned relief with having company as an in-law. Dad extended his arm around Orest's shoulder, asking, "You're not nervous now, are you, son?" He could not hide his happiness over "son" becoming more than an honorary term, as if that were the point of the day. On the other side, a mopey Catherine, burbling between Elizabeth and Aunt Cecilia. Mom and I stood silently, neither of us saying anything to the other. Whatever guidance she might have given to my sister on her wedding day certainly would not have applied to my situation. Better to keep quiet. Father Scanlon let out a series of "ahems." People in their places, the ceremony began.

Symbols. Relatives. Magnitude. Invocations and instruction. All surrounded me, yet I concentrated solely, strangely on a box. I could picture it, lodged in my head. My memory, I suppose. Before, everything through my eyes and ears would soak into tissue, into skin and cells, like water into the earth. Not then. I saw only the box. As Father Scanlon spoke and Catherine scowled and Dad beamed, I felt myself reaching out for a particle of each to store away. The interconnected right angles, with dimensions only so high and so wide and so deep. When filled to the very top, no more use for it. My body would decompose and perhaps the box would remain. Someone could pry open the lid and find this day and thousands more. To that person, the days would mean nothing.

With that, no more recording and cataloguing. I fixated on a nearby pillar. *Ivory and gold. It's ivory and gold*, I thought to myself. I was there, with my family, in the church, the dress tight against my waist, breath up through my body. In a few phrases, Orest Alworth had become my husband.

All but Father Scanlon returned to the house afterward. Other than two vases with flowers, no signs of a celebration, per my wishes. The positions around the table signaled the most noticeable alteration: Orest and I now sat next to one another, not at opposite corners. In my enclosed world, such a substantial shift.

The ordinary rhythm of our dinner discussions, disrupted due to wedding stress, resumed. Body clenches loosened. Rod-straight posture curved. Dad delivered a simple toast, not even to us as a couple: "To Amanda and Orest, may each of you continue to find happiness." Throughout the meal, I took in my family and, with some caution, Orest. Contentment. Whatever I had wanted, however blurry, perhaps had come into focus.

From Aunt Cecilia, something no one expected.

"Are we waiting until after dessert for gifts or can I give mine now?"

"Amanda said she didn't want any presents," Mom reminded her.

"I know, but she's my niece and whatever anyone says or doesn't say, it's her wedding day. So, I have something for her. It's my house."

A few disbelieving laughs followed. We awaited the actual, more practical announcement. Except no actual, more practical announcement came.

"It's my house. Don't get carried away. I'm not signing over the deed. I'm not that eccentric."

I hoped someone else would engage, but no one else could. "I don't understand, Aunt Cecilia." My nerves seemed to pump helium into my voice, making it high, scruffy.

"You live here. Orest lives at Mrs. Sullivan's. I live all alone. Plenty of room. No reason a husband and wife can't be under the same roof."

"Cecilia," Dad coughed.

"Separate rooms," she batted him away. "Separate rooms. Don't worry yourself."

I felt as if I were building a sandcastle in a hurricane. "Very kind of you, but we couldn't ask Orest to do that." Admittedly, the construction of my sentence, a bit passive and maybe even somewhat scheming.

"His wife a couple of hours and already making up his mind? Orest, what do you say?"

"I don't know." His answer slashed across my face, my cheeks drooping down, color draining onto my lap.

"Look, you're here. He's at the precinct or wherever he is most of the time. At my place, you can see each other. Or avoid each other. Whatever you want."

Not a sound.

"By the way, you're married," she added.

Still quiet.

"Look, I won't push."

"Why not?" Orest said. "What she says makes sense."

How I wished we had formed our own marital language of squints and blinks to relay true preferences, beyond the comprehension of onlookers.

"What will people say?" Dad asked.

"About a husband and wife living with an old woman?" Aunt Cecilia tore at his slapdash rationale. "Whatever they want, I guess."

"I need to think about it," I said. "We should talk about it later. Not now."

"Think and talk all you want. The house isn't going anywhere. Neither am I. Dessert?"

After a few awkward stops and starts, the conversation resumed, although without much energy. Aunt Cecilia's offer had emptied our reserves. We eventually gathered by the front door, unaware of how to end more than a dinner, but not quite a wedding. This point became even more peculiar as Orest prepared to depart without me. He and I approached one another with adolescent trepidation, the two of us seesawing from side-to-side. We hugged, released as quickly as entered. Pink-cheeked and speechless, Orest nodded and left, the rest of the family not far behind him. The door shut. Mom and Dad turned around. I already had started the climb to my bedroom to avoid their immediate ruling on the idea of Orest and I staying at Aunt Cecilia's house.

The next morning, my first as a sort-of wife, more questions, I knew. More time to talk about living arrangements and such. Not then. I wanted to enjoy the last minutes of my day. Untangled on the bed, I half-hoped I could fall asleep in my dress. A flash of pain through my abdomen sprang me upward.

It was happening.

CHAPTER NINE

Cecilia

My niece lied to me.

"Perfect," she told me.

"What do you think?" I asked Amanda about the bedroom I had laid out for her.

"Perfect," she said.

Liar.

I tell my fair share of lies, no doubt. Never do I judge a person for a bend in the truth from time to time. In fact, the more artful the lie, the greater my admiration. Curves, more interesting than straight lines, both on people and in stories. Amanda's lie bothered me, though, no matter how insignificant. If she had said, "pleasant," the word had a sharp enough edge. If she had said "yellow," deadpan in her delivery, I would have been subjected to that sardonic judgment of hers, which really was that sardonic judgment of mine. I had tutored her over the years, the two of us sitting together in the grandstand of wry observations during meals around the Bannon table.

The bedroom, I thought, had given Amanda so much to judge. I wanted to hear her tell me how the bedspread coughed up some moldy ginger scent, more sour than sweet. How the mattress was too tough and flat, fit only for a one-night guest. She might have said, "What a beautiful view," looking out the window at my pitiful backyard. "I see you have taken up gardening," she would have continued, ridiculing the patchy grass and ragged path that leads to the rusted, red birdbath.

Instead, Amanda said, "Perfect."

I hated that she used the word. Yes, hate. Not dislike or disappointment. Hate. Hated how she had stopped being the niece I knew, at least since the wedding. Even before the wedding. I had hoped the event itself, once over, might have let her relax, drop the weight behind her. Not at all. Only less and less like herself. I had witnessed this before, too many times. Spirited, defiant friends had pledged to remain themselves until death. Once married, the transformation, the destruction, the shrinking and the silence. They could not even see the changes, so I would have to point them out. They would defend themselves by assaulting me, such a masculine tactic.

"Better than being alone."

"We all can't afford to stay children."

These friends, at least, were fires that had died out somewhat slowly, over years and years in chill and neglect. Amanda was a flame blown out in an instant. Yes, maybe part of me believed I could strike a match by getting her out of that house. A flame, after all, needs oxygen and space. Amanda did not have much of either under the watch of her parents. Margaret knew this, too.

"I don't know any other way to say it," she told my niece when she decided to take me up on my offer, "but you're not well. None of us know how you'll hold up. We don't know what to expect. Things could happen quickly. You'll need—"

"My mother," Amanda interrupted.

"Your family," Margaret corrected. "I was going to say your family."

I tried not to take offense at the suggestion I was not enough family for her. I tried. A crafty strategy by her mother, to give credit where credit is due. Amanda had not spent more than a few nights outside her home over nineteen years. Even then, always with some other Bannon. Margaret trusted her daughter would miss something and this missing would return her to the house sooner than later. She might miss her room or miss knowing where to find her books. Or the noise of her father rumbling about, of her sister fighting every request and rule. Maybe Amanda would miss those cracks that pulled along the perimeter of the dining-room ceiling. Or that water stain in the bathroom or some other flaw.

As for me, I already missed my niece. I wanted her back before I would have to spend the rest of my life missing her.

"When does he move in?" Catherine asked, all of us—except Orest—around the dining-room table on the first night her sister would come stay with me.

Amanda did not answer, did not even look up from her plate. She wanted to deny her interest in him, I assumed. A little too late for that, it seemed to me. I finally had to say, "When he settles his affairs at Mrs. Sullivan's."

What swam madly inside that aloof, tin-can shell I once called my niece, I did not know. On our walk back to my house, even with her so distracted, I tried to find out.

"They still don't understand," I said, at first low, without my lips moving, hiding my words from Joseph and Margaret, who watched us from the front steps. "I'm not saying I do. Not entirely. But I think I understand better than they do. Everything fell into place for the two of them. I'm not saying that's bad. It's just that when it all comes together so easily, you don't even realize you're making a choice. But you are. If you want to know about choices, ask someone without options. They see it all coming together or falling to pieces better than anyone."

Amanda hummed and *hmmm*-ed acknowledgment, cordial and faraway.

"Think you'll be able to fall asleep in the new house tonight?"

"Doubtful. I haven't slept much for a while."

I started singing, mimicking an exaggerated, operatic baritone.

"When you're lying awake, with a dismal headache and repose is taboo'd by anxiety. I conceive you may use, any language you choose to indulge in, without impropriety. For your brain is on fire, the bedclothes conspire—"

"Aunt Cecilia, please stop."

"You don't like Gilbert and Sullivan?"

"I'm just … No, not now, I don't. I'm sorry."

"You apologize too much. You've got nothing to apologize for."

"I don't know about that."

"I do. I stopped apologizing thirty years ago. Maybe that explains why I live alone."

"I don't know about that, either."

"Don't get me wrong. I had options. I tell myself I did. I look at my friends. Some just went along with it all. I'd say they settled. That's probably the jealous part of me, the part that always has to win."

Amanda did not respond.

"I wish they would've written a song about me," I said.

"Gilbert and Sullivan?"

"Sure. Anyone, really. Don't you think I'd make a good subject?"

She titled her head a bit. Looked enough like a nod to me.

"I sometimes write it out in my head. Not the music. Just the lyrics. I would need help with the music. Maybe both. Keep trying to come up with something that rhymes with 'big flash of crazy.' Because that's the way people would describe me. I get stuck on lazy and hazy. Sounds forced and amateurish, no?"

"Daisy," she said. "Glazy?"

"See? Not easy."

"Maybe you should use a different word."

"No, that's my word, for better or worse. And I say better." We arrived at my house. I stopped before letting us in. "When time is actually slipping away, you don't even notice. But before you know it, you go from asking when something will happen to building a life around how it hasn't. It's not overnight. No." I unlocked the door and pushed it open. "Not even a week or a month. More like two years. Yes, I'd say about two years."

Once inside, Amanda went straight for the stairs. I had not finished. Some last-chance distress croaked up in my throat, freezing her on the third step. "You get comfortable with it all. And you make crazy remarks, because people pay attention. And you make even crazier remarks, because you don't want them to stop paying attention. If they did ... I don't know. So, that's what you become. A big flash of crazy. And that's why it would have to be in my song. What would you want in yours?"

Her face craned over her right shoulder. "I don't know," she said.

"I think someone should write one for you. It would be a good song. Probably a great one. But they would have to figure out how to rhyme with courageous. Harder than crazy."

"Contagious," she said. "Outrageous."

"Maybe not so hard, then."

Amanda continued up to her "perfect" bedroom. One day, I hoped she would return to the conversation, unpacking and shaking out my mishmash of insight and reflection. Not then, though. The prospect of Orest's arrival, no doubt, occupied her. After about thirty minutes downstairs, I headed up to my own bedroom. Assumed he would not show up that evening. No need to wait for him. About thirty minutes after that—

Bang. Bang. Bang.

I knew my house's clanging diction. The pipe sobs and floorboard yawns. I knew those beats came from the front door. Up from the bed, I blitzed into the hall. Amanda stuck her head out of her room.

"Stay here," I said. "I'll take care of it."

Down the stairs. Waiting by her bedroom door, Amanda must have heard the blend of my garbled speech with footsteps, pieces of a sentence breaking through: "... when to expect you. Certainly not now, but we're ready for you."

With a heavy tug at the banister, I pulled myself forward, Orest and his bags behind me. "I think you two know one another," I said, catching my breath.

Amanda drew her mouth into itself. Not quite a smile. Not really a grimace. Orest would have had to decide what it was.

"Sorry to be so late," he said. "I told Mrs. Sullivan I would be out this afternoon. I was delayed."

"Not to worry. We just got home ourselves. Right, Amanda?"

Nothing between them. I cranked out in a dreary monotone, "Let me show you where you'll stay."

I took Orest to the room facing the top of the staircase. The heavy, careless dump of his luggage shook the floorboards.

"If you don't mind waiting out there for a minute," I told him, "I just need to fix a few things in here."

Orest obeyed. Out in the hallway, with only the two of them, a stall. Someone or something always had done the hard work for them. Not then. Just a stall, each guarding the entrances of the rooms. Finally, my niece said something, if not quite the right thing.

"We didn't know when you would arrive."

"Is that a problem?" he said.

"No, not at all. Just a question."

"It was a statement."

It felt as if a sharp knife had cut open the glass of every window in the house, the March night jetting inside, icing over the three of us. I would have to do the hard work for her. Stepped back out and said, "The bathroom's next to you. She's in there. I'm at the end. It's starting to get warmer, so I don't think you'll need another blanket. Any questions, ask your wife. It'll give you two a reason to talk."

"Aunt Cecilia," Amanda chided.

"Teasing. Teasing," I rocked her side-to-side in an overdone embrace. "I'm going to bed. The house is yours."

At my door, I could not help myself. Threw back a look and said, "Been a long time since a man stayed here, but maybe not as long as you think."

Embarrassment brushed across their faces. Exactly as intended.

"I'm sorry," I heard Amanda say. "I would like to say you become used to it, but you don't."

"I've learned to appreciate her."

And that was it for the night. As I said, I knew the clanging diction of my house. Rapid thunks against the floor, perhaps purposefulness. A modest delay between steps, pensiveness, the mass of a concern bearing down on a person. Those early moments were studded with the shrill shove of drawers, restless rolls in bed, intermittent coughs. The minutes extended and extended into pure quiet.

Orest left before Amanda or I woke the next morning. He returned after eleven in the evening, the front door's whiny yap informed me. Amanda must have drawn up quite the storyline in her head. Because her head was drawing up a storyline, no doubt. Images of her husband pounding the Newark streets, waiting for an hour when the two of us had gone to bed. The soft click of his closing door signaling his invisibility, solitude, separation.

I wanted my niece to charge in there, to stop being so timid, to unload everything in her mind. Anger or desire or frustration. But no. Cowardice or convention or ambivalence held her back. She would not approach him that night or any other night. She likely spent her evenings recording his disquiet, his noises. Not what I had in mind for the two of them. It would have to do. They had so few chances to interact in the daytime.

Orest adhered to his early exits and late returns. Amanda still worked at Saint Barnabas, although the days there started to wind down. He attended dinner at Joseph and Margaret's only one or two times during the first week or so after settling in. Those occasions ended with the three of us walking down Pennsylvania Avenue, united only by our destination. I spoke. Amanda pretended to listen. Orest placed his thoughts where neither of us could locate them. At my house, we each immediately retired to our respective rooms.

What went on inside my home, the rest of the family must have wondered. No direct questions, no "How are things with Orest?" inserted casually into a conversation. Just side-to-side stares tracking the couple's few public appearances. I saw Tom and Elizabeth's suspicions play out in private looks to one another. I saw the fussy crease set in the bridge of Margaret's nose. I wanted to tell all of them to knock it off. Would not have done any good, though. Only Joseph brought up Orest with Amanda one evening in early April.

"I'm glad you're here," he said, returning from the precinct. She was setting places in the dining room. I sat in the living room. "Any plans for Orest's birthday?"

I could read the thoughts above my niece's head, her expression a little empty: *His birthday? He would have one, no?*

"It's the ninth," he added.

I had to commend Amanda. She told a beautiful, curvy lie. For the first time in weeks, she was herself.

"I know," she said, confidence stiffening her neck, elevating her chin. "We talked about it the other night."

"About what?"

"About what?" She began to unfurl a delicately woven tapestry as she kept knitting it. Impressive. "About his birthday. You know how Orest is, Dad. Doesn't want anyone to know. Doesn't want anyone mentioning it, much less doing anything."

Her conviction forced his acceptance. I honestly questioned how the man ever survived so long—much less excelled—as a police officer.

"I understand how he feels," he said. He moved toward the stairs and—for a second—snatched back the relief sinking into his daughter. "Don't you think we should do something?"

"Adamant, Dad. He was adamant. Didn't want it mentioned."

"You're his wife."

She was his wife. And she might finally have believed as much. Over dinner, then on our walk home, I could see her mind puzzling, trying to work out the problem. I loved it. When she asked me what to do, I had only one answer.

"A cake."

"A cake?" she repeated. I could hear her internal cry of "Avalanche!" as mountains of faith crashed down on top of her.

"A meal is too long," I said, "especially for you two. A present? You'd get it wrong. Even if you knew exactly what he needed, you'd get it wrong. Just bake him a cake. Thoughtful. Personal. Fast. And if that goes wrong, you still get to have cake."

Reluctantly, she followed my advice. I saw how the act of baking discomforted her. The kitchen's confines and heat tightened her collar, which she plucked out with her index finger over and over again, like some sort of tic. Domesticity must have felt like an invisible monster that bear-hugged her waist from behind, her legs kicking in the air as she tried to break free. How close she must have come to throwing *Mrs. Curtis's Cook Book* into the oven and serving him its ashes. Eventually, she calmed down. Back to basics. One cup of this. Two teaspoons of that.

When the night of April ninth arrived, Amanda waited alone for Orest. I went "out," the location purposely vague. I wanted my niece's creative powers to send me to venues more glamorous than reality. (I visited my friend's home, a few blocks away, for a game of cards.) I suspected those minutes unwound like rumpled wire for Amanda. The house vacant, the space probably seemed filled with spectators, all from her past. All of them staring down on her, gawkers to what would follow.

CHAPTER TEN

Orest

I wished they already were in bed. Or at least still at the Bannon's home.

Thirty yards. I had to clear about thirty yards—from right inside the house to the bedroom—without either of them noticing me. Over the weeks, I had counted in my head the number of seconds from when my key turned the lock to the clack-close of the bedroom door. Eleven seconds. I could have done it in four or five, but I had to set the right pace. Could not sprint, because it would have appeared awkward. They would have known I did not want to see them. They already knew, though. At least Cecilia did. She had me figured out most nights, no matter how quickly or how slowly I walked.

"Trying to avoid me?" she would say, either sitting in the living room or standing outside her bedroom.

"No, I didn't want to wake you."

"I've heard that one before. I know when a man's trying to avoid me."

She was right.

On that night, before I stepped inside, I inhaled and started the count. *One. Two. Three.* Before I could reach four—and the seventh stair—I heard, "Orest."

Amanda, not Cecilia, waited in the living room.

Without making eye contact, I asked, "Something wrong?" in my work-day voice, the one I believed I had crated up for the day.

"I'm sorry. If I—"

"Is there?"

"No. Not at all. Nothing at all."

"If it's nothing, then—" The sentence, I did not bother to finish. I continued upstairs.

"Orest." Her volume, unnecessarily high, irritatingly so.

My eyelids shut for three seconds. Another deep breath. Patience gathered. I faced her. She did not speak, instead walking into the dining room, out of my view. A rather unassertive request for me to join her, I assumed. I followed. She stood by the far-end head, near the kitchen entrance, the full length of the table between us. In the center, a cake.

"Is that what you wanted to show me?"

"Yes."

"Why?"

"It's your birthday."

Such quiet between us. All I ever desired, quiet between us. Once I had this quiet, no idea what to do. Amanda chose not to explain. I must have looked like a horizon set to thunder down. Certainly felt like one.

"How did you know?"

"My father."

"He shouldn't have said anything."

"It's just a cake," she said, airy, confident.

My fingers curled around the back of the dining-room chair. Would have broken it in pieces, if nudged only a bit more. "You had no right to do this."

"No right?" she said. "I'm your—"

"My what?" I moved counterclockwise around the table, Amanda traveling in the same direction, at the same speed, the two of us fixed objects on a dumbwaiter. "My what? You're my what?"

"Your wife."

"My wife?"

"Yes. I'm your wife."

My bottom teeth stuck out, catching and slowing each word: "You only wanted to get married."

"And you agreed."

I turned to leave the room and the argument.

"See?" She tagged after me. "You know you did."

"You're dying," I yelled, my back bowed, wrists turned in, hands clawed.

The sound whammed throughout the house. A release, yes, but at all necessary? Cruel and gratuitous, perhaps. The corners of her mouth snuck upward in a slight, satisfied smile, as if she had gotten from me exactly what she had sought. My outburst made her stronger. I became weaker.

"Amanda, I—"

"No. You're right."

She did not shatter. Stony and reasonable, she discharged all drama from the room. "This was ridiculous. The cake. The wedding. I'm moving back home. You can move out. Whenever best for you."

"Amanda, I—"

"Please," she said. She pitied not herself, but me. "I'm sorry about all of it. You shouldn't feel bad. I just feel … I just feel silly. I never feel silly, so I want to go to bed." Halfway up the stairs, she leaned over the banister and told me, "The cake is still yours, if you want it."

Her plan might have worked. One way or another, she had forced us to have an honest conversation. Ugly and awful and thorny, but honest, however brief. I remained downstairs at first. I dropped piles "Damn it" all over the living-room floor for nearly an hour. Only a cake, after all. I would have escaped, if I could. Not the house, but the city, the state. Gone somewhere beyond my mistakes. Toronto. Maybe Kansas City. A place to begin again. I could have banged on her door, apologized. What would I even have apologized for? For telling the truth? The truth does not become any more or any less itself over time. Amanda seemed to know this, maybe better than anyone. Brush it up. Hide it, like everything else. Examine it from over there or up here. Does not matter. The truth stays the same. But you can hate the truth. And I hated it, the regret blathering in my head. Finally upstairs, I stuck myself on the bed, my right forearm pressed to my skull, knees bent. Not comfortable.

Did not want comfortable. If I had slept one full minute, I could not remember, could not feel those seconds in my ankles, in my elbows, underneath my eyes.

I left even earlier than usual the next morning. On the job, my mind grinded over the prior night. The situation called for something bigger and heavier than an apology. Atonement, perhaps. The word seemed powerful and ominous and religious in a way I did not fully understand.

Late in the afternoon, I ran across the blocks between the precinct and Pennsylvania Avenue. Nervous pedestrians might have thought a police emergency had occurred. I had to see my wife, if I even could call her that name after the last evening. Her family already might have heard. Her bags already might have been packed and moved.

On the steps of the Bannon home, I huffed and gulped, a sweat patch on the back of my shirt. I knocked. Not yet enough of a family member to enter on my own. The Captain opened the front door. His face looked as if dunked in a hot, gray wax. Inside, a numbing tableau. I sorted the evidence. Catherine on Mrs. Bannon's lap, head in her mother's chest. Tom and Elizabeth, shaken, intertwined on the couch. I drew a terrible conclusion. Even more so when the Captain put his hand on my shoulder.

"We have some bad news, son."

I considered the worst. Amanda then walked in from the direction of the kitchen.

"I'm afraid it's Cecilia."

CHAPTER ELEVEN

Amanda

On the morning of Aunt Cecilia's funeral, I turned on my side in bed, still in the room in her house. I did not think of her, sorry to say. I thought of my parents. Only a few homes away, both likely awake well before dawn, neither one wanting the other to know. Mom probably could not stomach another, "How are you?" or, "Everything all right?" from Dad, especially then. She might have thought to herself: *If he truly cared about the answer, he would know enough not to ask the question.* Aunt Cecilia's death had transformed abstraction into reality for Mom. So many plans and rituals. Plans and rituals, repeated soon enough.

My father probably focused on something inconsequential, like the bedroom ceiling. *Needs painting,* he might have thought. He also might have reviewed in his head the bill from Callan and Matthews Funeral Home. And he would have hated himself. Preparations. Casket. Miscellaneous. *Remember the numbers,* he might have reminded himself. For a comparison. Might as well have requested a discount, assuring them, "We'll be back."

Some grim rites Aunt Cecilia's stroke had initiated. Dad likely inhaled deeply, battling against gravity and age to sit upright. My mother maybe pulled the blanket tight over her right ear and around the top of her forehead. A few centimeters down and she could have suffocated away all that would follow. Instead, she might have delayed in bed, a late start that would have given her an excuse to rush past my father and that one question: *How will we then?*

I felt Aunt Cecilia's absence in her house, of course. I realized how much one person adds to an enclosed space. How much heat she had generated, because it suddenly was cold. How without her everyday motions circulating air, rooms smelled dank and musty. How she must have soaked up the silence, because the quiet seemed like rising water that could drown me. I considered what I might contribute to a space. And if anyone would notice the changes I would leave behind.

When we sorted through the dresses in Aunt Cecilia's closet to select one for her burial, we spread the choices out on the bed, the rancid fragrance of expired perfume in the air, as if her memory already had started to decay. Which one? Which one? The question no one could voice practically wrote itself out above Mom's and Elizabeth's heads: *Which one for Amanda?*

Which one for me, indeed. I tried to come up with a tension-bursting pun, but failed. I felt like a ghost right then in that room. Even more so when reading my aunt's death notice in the *Newark Evening News.*

Mine would seem so unfinished, depressing a reader who never had met me. The person would think: *Only nineteen. (Maybe twenty.) So young.*

I bled into the ceremony, I knew. Diluted the grief. Only I could mourn without diversion, the others allotting some percentage of their sadness to anticipation. I carried with me to Aunt Cecilia's funeral the responsibility of pure bereavement. Inside my parents' home, foggy-windowpane expressions greeted me. No one looked me in the eye. Only a vacant browse at a far-too-familiar picture or a nervous search in a bag.

On the walk to the church, the April rain held off, perhaps paying its respects. Sunlight fringed Saint Columba's in ecclesiastical grandeur, a theatrical touch Aunt Cecilia surely would have mocked. She also would have bragged about how friends and neighbors crowded over half the pews, about how Father Scanlon moved the service along at a brisk tempo, a tribute to her impatient nature.

The burial at Holy Sepulchre took place after the mass. The warmer temperature firmed the soggy earth, so we could walk the grounds in our fancy, heeled shoes without stumbling much. I suspected that, once home, everyone else would wash off the mud caked along the soles, worried cemetery soil could infect them to an untimely end. Elegiac. The images made me remember the word elegiac from school, from Tennyson and Whitman and Coleridge, I thought. Tears dripped off Mom's and Elizabeth's and Catherine's faces, landing on the grass. The casket. The open ground. The rows of headstones. Felt myself dragged, as if by an undertow, to reflection.

My last place. Never to leave. My family would visit me. On my birthday. Some holidays. At least at first. They eventually would stop. Maybe once a year or so. When they were guilty. Catherine, when she grew old, looking back. Nieces and nephews told they had another aunt. She died young.

Solemnity, itself, shoved at the soft backside of my skull, chin pressed into my breastbone. Eyes up from the tilted-down mourners, I surveyed the property. Tried to commit the broadest and smallest details to memory. No chance to return. Aunt Cecilia might have taken me, if I had asked, but she got there before me.

Swept it all up. Near a tree? Neighbors? Who would be the neighbors? Whose family members would read my gravestone? In twenty … thirty … eighty years, who would stop to read the dates, that thin dash that was my life? Where would I be? On a bend, with rainwater rushing over? Would I feel it? Feel any of it? The sunlight? The shade? The snow?

The questions struck fast at the back of my knees. I buckled and slumped forward almost to ninety degrees. No one noticed, all suspended in their heartache. Arms crossed around my abdomen. Illness? Sadness? Fear? None of them? All of them? Did not know. The loss of control, stabbing and scraping at my stomach wall. With heavy whiffs, I stabilized. The discomfort remained, though. More. I needed something more from the day, from the scene. A picture. Had to have a definite picture of whatever insignificant tract I would occupy. The unknown would become more of an obsession than I could manage. And obsession already had taken enough of my days.

A warbled, incoherent blessing from Father Scanlon concluded the formalities, as if a hypnotist had snapped his fingers and released us from a spell. The group expanded slowly and slowly, until fading as a single mass. I let the muddle hide me and lead me to the small, serious, bird-boned man in the bark-brown suit who circled the perimeter. He held documents against his chest with his left arm, while with his right he directed the staff about those tasks no one wishes to see. I approached him.

"Do you work here?"

"Mr. Reilly, assistant director. My condolences." Soft-spoken, he relaxed me, the talent of a good person or a person good at his job. Either would do.

"Can you help me? I would like to find a plot, one not yet—"

"In service? Of course. Please give me the name. I'll take a look at our records. We'll schedule a time next week."

"Next week?" A wholly other sound exploded through the words, the "K" crackling high into the air. Mr. Reilly knew I measured my time in units smaller than weeks.

"Let me see what I can do. What's the name?"

"Bannon. It should be under Joseph and Margaret."

His left arm lowered, the clumsy stack of papers seemingly one with him, an appendage linked by unseen veins and vessels. Thumbed through the pages, his eyes side-to-side, up-and-down. I looked over my shoulder at the dwindling crowd, so concerned Dad or Elizabeth or nosey Catherine might come over and spoil the plan: "Time to leave, Amanda."

"Found it. We're in luck. Not too far away. Not far at all."

Mr. Reilly led me about twenty yards northeast of Aunt Cecilia's site. We stopped at an undistinguished, lightly populated section, neighbored by a handful of headstones in varying sizes and shapes.

"The Bannon plot sits about here," he said, drawing a rectangle in the air with his hand. "Need a better map for an exact location."

I expected the scene to overtake me, for the earth to tear at my heart so hard I would have broken ribs, my head in a seizure-trance, lunging through the decades. I felt nothing. I took note of the nearest tree, how the terrain fell flat, how the sun—then directly over-head—neglected not an inch. Mr. Reilly understood what he witnessed. Not his first time. A little under one minute, I arched my eyebrows and let out a philosoph-ical breath. We began our walk back toward the others.

"Thank you," I said.

"Of course, Miss Bannon."

No reason to correct him. None at all.

"Actually, it's Mrs. Alworth."

"My apologies."

"Not to worry. I'm barely used to it myself."

After a few more steps, he said, "We have some Alworths here, too. Name sticks in my mind. It's near the front of our files. Try to keep track of the names. Getting harder over time."

His parents.

I counted the expense of further delay. Worth the risk, worth testing my family's patience. I touched Mr. Reilly's arm, so out of character.

"I'm sorry. One more favor. The Alworths, can you show me? Michael and Ellen. My husband's parents."

"Mrs. Alworth," he said, his tongue pressed against his bottom teeth, my name a hiss.

"Please." I hoisted the plea so high above our heads, had he not accepted, it would have fallen and smashed like a ceramic plate. Again, he maneuvered his left arm into an "L"-shaped easel, the papers propped up. His index finger ran under a series of lines. "It's a bit of a walk."

What would I learn from a piece of etched stone? Such a distortion, really, to search among the dead for some connection to the living. The day had become so warm, I regretted the decision with each yard. A fitting reminder, though. Could have just curled up, back at my spot, staying there in perpetuity, saving everyone the trouble of having to move me one day soon. Mr. Reilly slowed down, examined the inscriptions.

"The Alworths," he called out, then receded.

I neared the grave. No reason for nerves. I would leave no impression. They would pass no judgment. Whatever sensation had eluded me minutes earlier suddenly hit. The moment, nearly sacramental, chrism coating the inside of my skin. Steadied myself with a hand on the headstone. Deliberately pored over the engraving, as if my intensity somehow honored two strangers. As I read, my world stopped.

Ellen Alworth died on April ninth, 1897.

Michael Alworth died on April tenth, 1897.

Everything became all-the-less and all-the-more mysterious.

Only one person could tell me the truth.

CHAPTER TWELVE

Amanda

Back at my family's house, friends and neighbors traded stories about Aunt Cecilia. Everyone half-expected her to walk through the front door, shake free of grave dirt and join the festivities. She would have heard herself recalled as a series of sarcastic, firecracker vignettes. Exactly as she had told me: a big flash of crazy. A humbling reward, I suppose, to be proved correct on such a matter, even for the dead.

Mom, Elizabeth, Catherine and I hustled between the kitchen and dining room. Full dish out, empty dish in. Full dish out, empty dish in. Tried to outwork my sisters. I had to address every possible duty my mother could assign. When she said, "That should do it for now," I was off. The inviting weather matched with the uninviting crowd would have sent my father outside. There, I found him, leaning by the front steps, a swarm of simplicity in his head.

"Caught me. Needed some air."

The phrase, his standard excuse. Extended his right arm toward me, a gesture he did not make that often. I pressed against his frame. My muscles began to relax, the urgency behind what I had to say escaping my body.

"Too bad Orest couldn't come," he said. "Cecilia was fond of him."

The name, a command. I saw no clearer path.

"Dad, about Orest—"

"Expected this," he said. "About your living arrangement, we—"

"What? No. Not that."

"It might not be best for the two of you—"

"Dad," I said, wriggling free.

"Something wrong?"

"No." I reconsidered. "Yes." He looked confused. I could not be tentative. "It's about his parents. Orest's parents."

The slight caving of his inside eyebrow corners converted confusion into animosity. "What about his parents?" His words, no longer crooning and affable. He distinctly pronounced every syllable for emphasis. My father had departed the scene, replaced by Captain Bannon, a persona he called on to intimidate, to restore order.

"You never told me what happened to them."

"You're right. I didn't."

"I thought I should know, since—"

"Since why? You thought you should know what, Amanda?" His temple veins ballooned. His voice, as if cooked in a boiler kept deep in a dungeon. I had sliced open a nerve. Had to keep digging.

"I thought I should know if Orest's mother died giving birth to him."

The sentence fell hard. A strong gust could not have blown it away. Landed not with a crash, but a thump. The next line fell even harder.

"And if his father took his own life the next day."

Dad rubbed his right hand against his forehead, then down the full length of his face, pulling and screwing his chin. He spun in a short, lost stagger, untangling himself from invisible cables, holding his fist as high as his head. He halted a few steps away from me and said in a whisper more violent than a shout: "You clever girl. You have to be so damn clever, don't you? You can't leave things alone. You never could."

I remained still, solid.

"Never say another word of this again," he pointed his right index finger at me. "Understand? Do you understand?"

I answered with a quick turn and to-hell-with-you march into the house. My footsteps up the staircase banged a loud, one-two beat. Into my bedroom, where I so often had reassembled myself. Avoided the window-sill, not risking even a glance outside at Dad. On my bed, on my side, bent like a sickle, a few tears crossed the plain of my nose, off the tip, staining the comforter. No emotion behind them. A physical cleansing. Water spilling from gutters after a storm.

Nearly an hour later, my door opened. No knock. My father walked in. I sat up. The two of us, without the slightest resemblance to one another, set our faces into identical expressions: wounded and combative, equally prepared for a truce or a fight. Neither one of us apologized. He put his hands in his pockets, dumped his eyes into the floor.

"I'm going to tell you things, things I've never told anyone," he began. His voice hiked higher. His syllables trembled. I almost could hear the frantic ellipses between his thoughts, a radio signal scratching across the frequency in search of a steady, calm buzz.

"Because if I don't tell you—knowing you—you'll keep looking. You probably would be able to put some of it together, because you're so smart."

He had downgraded "clever" to "smart," but it still stung.

"And you would start asking questions, but no one else knows the answers. Not your mother. Not a priest. No one. And I don't want you asking these questions, especially not of Orest. It's all been long settled. There's no point in bringing it up. What I say can't leave this room."

"Dies with me," I said humorlessly.

"If you went looking, you probably would come across Mike's death certificate. You would see the signature of a man named Taylor. He was from Mullins' Morgue. He drank too much and owed us more favors than he could repay. He died a few years after all of this, so he would be no good to you. You also would see my name. I'm listed as the informant. Sounds ominous, no?"

The edges of his consonants were sanded down a bit. He slowly reclaimed the character I knew. He wandered in slender ovals. He occasionally looked in my direction. A confession, not a conversation.

"Ellen, her death certificate was straightforward. Straightforward and sad. She died in childbirth, like you guessed. Complications. Strange word, complications. Almost condescending coming from a doctor, as if I wouldn't understand the real reason, so there's no point in telling me. Whatever it was—too much bleeding, weak heart—didn't really matter. She was pretty, fun and happy one day, then gone the next."

I adjusted upright, toward the front of the bed. Few daughters ever hear their father's darkest secrets. My thumbs twitched.

"So, Ellen's was straightforward. Mike's was, too. Coronary thrombosis. That's the cause of death. Written on that document by Taylor himself. Coronary thrombosis. I don't have to tell you what that is. Thinking you're about to be a father, then you lose your wife. Too much on a heart, right?"

Dad paused, his eyes around the room. He hushed, because if he spoke too loudly, he might have awakened someone long gone, someone who either could tell or hear the truth.

"When I found him at his house over on Front Street, on the floor of his bedroom, it made sense. His heart just couldn't take it. Because if that's not what had happened, it could've meant something different. Do you understand? It could've meant headlines in newspapers. It could've meant Mike and Ellen not being buried together. And we couldn't have that, could we? So, it was a coronary thrombosis. A broken heart.

Nothing else. People accepted it. No one asked questions. They had the decency not to back then."

He made "decency" sound like pure profanity.

"I shouldn't say everyone accepted it. Mike's sister didn't. I didn't even know he had a sister until she showed up at the hospital to claim the baby. So odd he never said anything about her. She was calm and cruel. Only spoke five words: 'My brother sent for me.' Strange, right? He sent for her. Before he died, he sent for her, this woman he never bothered to tell us about. She didn't look even a little bit sad. More aggravated than anything. I saw she was too smart and too terrible to believe coronary thrombosis. She took the baby with her to wherever she lived, not far from Philadelphia, I think. That was it. Didn't even stay for the funeral."

"Orest doesn't know?" I asked, one of dozens of questions in my brain, ready to gush out my eye sockets. Had to prioritize. Once through the doorway, Dad never again would acknowledge the topic.

"Whatever he knows, he knows. Whatever he doesn't, he doesn't. I'm not going to tell him. Neither are you. I've only said how much his parents meant to me. That's the truth. The rest doesn't matter."

But it did matter, I realized. I could see the "rest" all around my father. Sat on his lungs, refusing him air. The "rest" had broken the prism filtering his decisions, had destroyed the iron railings keeping him in the lane of consistency. Sorrier and sorrier for him, I felt.

"I'm just glad I'm the one who found him. Mike had a bad day."

Dad scattered behind a quarter-century of secrets and supposed sins, memories that cut deep, undetectable scars. His tidy moral metrics could not have accounted for complexity. Loyalty and despair and weakness and benevolent deceit could not exist in a single act, a single imperfect moment. He had to apply his most elementary calculus: perpetrators lurk behind evil. Blame must be assigned. With no suspects available, Dad convicted himself. For what crime? Friendship? Human frailty?

The sun dipped from view, my bedroom glowing in amber. Only a few hours ruptured by so much consequence: Aunt Cecilia's funeral, the discovery at Holy Sepulchre, the confrontation with Dad, his ultimate revelations. Over recent months, I had experienced a terminal diagnosis, an unexpected marriage. This day, though, this day would hover above all others.

Connection. Dad and I finally had achieved a connection. Crossed a lifetime of distance in one exchange. I knew more of him than anyone else on earth. Months or years later, when I would be long gone, he would remember what he had shared and it might bring him some consolation.

Orest. Did he know? Possibly. Sleepless, compulsively amending Orest, casting himself as the villain. Still, did he carry this knowledge? Something different. Not certain.

Our marriage? Over. Right? Was there suddenly potential not there the day before? I possessed a secret, itself a perverse pleasure. I could wield such influence, but I had to resist. Something more, though, could be done for him. What?

The answers, not in that room. Before the day lost all light, I had to return to Aunt Cecilia's house. One night with my family, back in their home, would have set an irreversible course. Protests over my departure awaited me. And the darkness or some other frivolous element could tip the scales against me. I walked down the stairs and took in everyone: exhausted, each minute of the day stacked on top of them. I said confidently, permitting no ground for debate, "If you don't need anything else, I'll go back."

The room jolted with an uneasy energy. Dazed victims simultaneously coming-to after an accident. Mom and Dad traded I-thought-you-handled-it looks. Tom shifted in his chair. No one spoke, each perhaps curious if the flexibility of "back" would bend upstairs or down the street. Three steps ahead of disapproval, I exited, the group disabled by disbelief.

Fear fueled my tear down Pennsylvania Avenue. The clog of street noise in my ears, plausible deniability for not listening to cries of "Amanda!" that could have tracked me. Aunt Cecilia's house loomed like an asylum, curtained in lavender, gothic light. Once inside, I propped my back against the front door. A quick, illicit thrill sizzled up my body. I had one night.

Time and location do alter perspective, I recognized as I prepared for bed. Maybe because the window in the bedroom of my parents' house faced a setting sun, notions of renewal simmered. But in the seclusion and dimness of the back bedroom in Aunt Cecilia's home, fewer and fewer possibilities. With that, my more rational self began to count the evening there as my last, my last with Orest in the bedroom next door.

Near ten, I heard the familiar bars of his return: the gradual progression of quarter notes up the staircase, building to the shut of his door. A prolonged rest and something so unexpected: a knock.

"Amanda."

Up from the bed—with a check in the mirror—I opened the door.

"Is something wrong?" I asked.

He waited, his eyes nabbing clues from over my shoulder, then hiding in the crevices between the floorboards. "I didn't know if you would still be here."

"Is that a problem?"

"No."

The person before me seemed different. The same angles to his face, the stiff part in his hair, but smaller, his confidence sapped by some sickness of conscience. His midsection rounded inward slightly, apologetically. Perhaps most out of character, he asked a question: "How was today?"

"Fine. Sad. Strange. I don't really know yet."

Simple, evening conversation, foreign to him. Fire to a neanderthal. For several seconds, we stood there, on opposite sides of the door. Finally, he said, "I'll probably be here a little while longer."

"It's not a problem."

"Would you stay?" he shot back, loud and fast, a tight spiral pressed down and springing upward.

I could feel the skin under my eyes wrinkle, the lines in my forehead compressing, so perplexed. Was his question hypothetical? Direct? Contingent in some way? The answer was yes, regardless, but I hesitated. "Being in that house today," I began, faux world-wise, "I don't know if I want to go back yet. So, no, I wouldn't mind being here a little while longer."

"All right," he said. He backed away, a loose glacier lapping up a puzzling surf all over me. Had we arrived at an agreement? Or would he again bang on my door the next night to tell me he was uncertain I would be there?

A few feet away, his body in darkness, his voice reached out: "I thought tomorrow we could have dinner together. We could go out somewhere. I can be here at six, if that works for you."

CHAPTER THIRTEEN

Amanda

Life moves imperceptibly, I had come to believe. Minutes roll into hours. The hours build into days and weeks, piling into months and years. The accumulation, we call an existence, by default. Bursts of consequence—births, losses—maybe leave us a little more aware. All that occurred prior to these sparks seems only a prelude to living.

A tally of the mundane and the passive could have ground me into submission. The possibility for the extraordinary, perhaps that kept me going. The day of Aunt Cecilia's funeral might have been extraordinary. Given to me and taken from me. Deposits and withdrawals. What remained? Promise?

The next morning, I still had a husband, one who seemingly, surprisingly wished to continue living with me. Dad had told me such a sad story, one so incomplete. The loss of my aunt. All unavoidable reminders of fragility and transience.

Promise should have awaited me.

I felt dread.

Mom and Dad could ruin everything. "Home," they could demand. Surprise and fatigue aided my getaway for a single night. Not again. Daylight would have heated arguments sharpened over frustrated evening hours. ("Of course she has to come back here." "Why are you yelling at me? I agree with you.") Disobedience, I could pull off to some degree. A half-step here or there beyond the bounds drawn by my parents. What faced me this morning, though, would call for an epic resistance. Comply and leave Orest? Unthinkable, yet still quite possible.

The bed could swallow only so many of my worries. I could feed it not another minute. Mom's impatience soon would have sped up the block, abducted me, carried me back to the house. Blanket off, feet to the floor, reality's chill smacked me. Warmth scrammed from the mattress, the pillows. No rag-doll flop into the covers for a few more minutes. Dressed and ready, I brought with me not a single item more than I needed for the day. All would remain. I would not concede defeat. Not yet.

Inside my parents' home, no signs of the prior day's mourning. No errant, lipstick-ringed glasses about the side tables, abandoned by a get-them-tomorrow rationale. The setting had transitioned back without effort, disconcertingly so. *Will be the same for me*, I thought. In the kitchen, I hoped to see Catherine, even Elizabeth. Absence spoke of seriousness. Serious discussions always held alone, the other two sisters sent out. Only my mother.

"Good morning, Mom."

Not a word. Dishes and utensils, the victims of her aggression. I sat. She parked breakfast before me. The clank of the plate and cup flicked against my cranial nerves. She joined me. Her tone: tired, unsympathetic and direct.

"Amanda, after what happened to Aunt Cecilia, your father and I think you should move back home."

"I know." I bit my toast.

"You'll come home, then?"

Chewed quickly. Mouth open, right before another bite, I said, "Orest and I would like to stay there."

"You and Orest?" She repeated, distrust swelling in the question mark.

"Yes. We talked last night."

"I didn't realize the two of you were making decisions together." She folded and unfolded the napkin before her, aggravation in every crease. "I didn't realize the two of you were even speaking."

"We're married, Mom." I called on Aunt Cecilia's short, impertinent logic, as if she could swing the debate from underneath the soil of Holy Sepulchre.

"We didn't let you get married to give you an excuse to disobey us," my mother said. She did not respond well to rhetorical gamesmanship.

I felt myself slip into churlishness, a not-unfamiliar slide, powerless to resist. "I didn't realize you let me get married," I said in the slow staccato I used when underlining a point.

"That's not what I meant." Mom reached out for my hand, which I tucked into crisscrossed arms. "There were unusual circumstances. I didn't think it was a good idea for you to live there before, even with Aunt Cecilia. Never hid my feelings. She's gone now. It's important you stay here."

"Worried about what people will think? Tell them the truth. We're married."

"Don't confuse me with your father. I just don't want you to get hurt."

"Get hurt? Do you remember what started all of this? Anything I want. That's what I was told. Anything I want. This is what I want, so don't take it away from me. Don't go back on your promise."

"It wasn't my promise. And you don't have the right to demand and get everything you want. Every conversation can't end with you saying you're married, you're sick."

"But I am married. I am sick. And I am nineteen years old. These are my decisions. And don't insult me. I don't have to use guilt. My arguments aren't weak."

I bayonetted my mother with "weak." I wanted a fast win, even though victory was certain in my mind. Mom, so penned in by conformity, her backbone atrophied by deference, ultimately would give in, I believed. Or she would capitulate with some spiteful, I'll-show-you affirmation of personal autonomy. Either way, I would prevail, I knew. Only had to press a little. Did more than that.

"Mine are weak?" My mother's voice steamed the kitchen, the white tiles clamming, the wallpaper about to peel away at the hems. I thought she might have called up the memory of me as an infant, vulnerable and cooing with round cheeks and a soft, sprouted head. Or a vision of me at the end, sunken and emaciated, coughing away the last minutes of life. I think she only felt manipulation latching onto her, too feeble to pull it off. "You're so much smarter than everyone, aren't you? Always have been."

"Mom, one year from now, I promise you'll regret this."

"Regret what?"

"This. This conversation. This ridiculous objection. You will look back and wonder why you ever gave me such a hard time. You will. And you will realize it doesn't matter. Any objection doesn't matter."

"I thought you didn't have to use guilt."

"That's not guilt. It's the truth. One year from now, it will not matter that two people—two people who just so happen to be married—lived together in the same house for a few weeks before one of them died. It will not matter. But living there matters to me, right now. And it's not hurting anyone."

"It's hurting you."

"How?"

"He doesn't love you."

"I know," I shouted. A thunderclap, ending with an uppity, cigarette-smoke chuckle blown in her face.

My mother, stunned, kept slogging forward. "Amanda, you need to be with people who love you."

"That's your point? Because he doesn't love me and you do, I should live here? Because there are never any false moments in a marriage, are there? Never any of those moments when someone doesn't want to be somewhere else? I'm no expert. There must be some ratio or formula or proportion that makes a marriage legitimate. Does the number of minutes when you want to be married have to outweigh the number you don't? Is that how it works? But I wouldn't know anything about that from what I've seen."

Too far.

I had gone too far. Propriety. Honor. Filial piety. I had flattened those blockades to drive straight into the territory of "too far," a frigid ravine beyond the civilization of kitchens and living rooms. We both rasped the thin air, the only sound either of us could hear.

How to turn around and go back, I wondered.

Breed a survivor and you breed a monster, Mom probably thought.

"You're right," she spoke first, wiping her brow and stroking hairs in place, "you wouldn't know anything about that. You're also right: I'll regret this conversation. You have to ruin everything for the rest of us to get what you want. You always have."

She stood, picked up the dishes, over to the sink, back to the sanctuary of home-life habits. Her arms scrubbed frenetically. Mess would not triumph, no matter what else my mother might have lost that morning.

Alone with my presumptive, pyrrhic victory, I saw myself lean away from the table and fall backward into an emptiness, no floor to catch me, not even the sawdust and clutter of the basement. Only emptiness. The achievement cost me piece of myself, a piece my mother might have missed one day in the future, years from then. Perhaps no longer, which made me sad. A little-girl sad she usually would have eased by saying, "Everything is fine." No such comfort came my way. I said softly, "I will come home, Mom. I promise. Just not now."

Her eyes plugged up to the far corner of the ceiling. "I've let some cobwebs gather up there. Can't do with that." She returned to the dishes. "I suppose you would like me to tell your father."

"Yes."

"We'll do it together. Tonight. After dinner."

A few seconds passed. The pause, so conspicuous, almost tapped her on the shoulder.

"About dinner, Mom."

CHAPTER FOURTEEN

Amanda

Cakes, I could bake. Meals, not as well. The best I could do had gone untouched on the dining-room table several nights earlier. A restaurant would save me from a charade in the kitchen. The juggling of pans. The dashing of ingredients. I might have used this time to consider the outfit I would wear to dinner, but I could not. I cared less about appearance since Aunt Cecilia had died, even less so since the morning negotiation with my mother. Had to stand by the it-does-not-matter point with some consistency, both for living arrangements and attire. Care and concern, somewhat mutable, I had come to understand.

Inside the entryway of Aunt Cecilia's house, I waited. I thought less about Orest's arrival and more about my mother. Poor Dad. He had departed that morning supported by at least one ally in his prissy campaign. He would return to a home with a ceiling for a floor, the last-to-know soldier of a surrendered cause. I respected Mom's finesse in those situations. A tamer of wild animals, themselves clueless they had been tamed. *More*, I realized. She could have been *more*. The regret for thinking her weak tugged at the edges of my mouth.

As six o'clock clicked closer, my heart did not beat faster. My blood pressure did not rise. Sitting down, the upholstery began to meld with my exposed forearm skin, the chair drawing in my awareness of contrast and dimension and time. The scuff-pop of the front door rattled up through my skull, jogging loose instant-awake flares. *Where? Husband. Dinner.*

"I'm sorry I'm late. Your father always stresses punctuality."

I pulled myself together and up. "Don't let my mother hear you say that. His hypocrisy would land him next to Aunt Cecilia."

Orest did not seem to find me funny. I felt myself covered in his dopey skepticism, as if wit were a germ I had caught only that afternoon. "You can laugh," I almost told him, but I had not nearly enough stamina to begin the evening running backward. Of course, our evening appeared never set to begin. I envisioned some mammoth comma between us, one fattening up on my concern he did not remember why he had come home at that hour. Rather than remain there the entire night, I asked, "Should we eat?"

Out the door, onto the street, into a spring after-glow that welcomed us with warmth and noise, the first link in a chain of better days. Such a luxury, having somewhere to be on a weeknight, surrounded by those with the same gift. I could have walked from one end of the city to the other, to experience all in that moment, on that single day, because the next day, everything would be different. I wanted to know those differences, to own them. The beautiful ones and the ugly ones. I knew too much of the same. The same path from one house to the other. The same place at the table. The same faces and talk. I had with me now a husband, yes, but more importantly, I had before me something different. So distracted, I forgot to ask Orest where we would dine. Moving alongside him, the patter and beeps around us better than any conversation.

How far we had walked, I had not noticed. We passed suitable option after suitable option, until arriving at Childs on Market Street. Green-copper walls fanned to a high ceiling. Black, iron tables stuck up from a glimmering white floor. *A cathedral, not a restaurant*, I thought.

"Two, please," Orest said. With one number, he had joined us together. Such negligible nonsense, but a public statement. Drunk from the journey, I believed myself.

"Have you been here before?" I asked as we took our seats, leaping into the rushing river of dinner chitchat that babbled around us, hoping it would carry us to a painless discussion.

"No, someone from the precinct recommended it."

"That always works, except when it doesn't," I said with a put-on sophistication. "If you end up not liking where they suggested, when you see that person, you have to decide if you lie. For whatever reason, politeness absolves dishonesty."

Orest studied his menu. I studied him.

"If it's a special occasion and it goes wrong," I continued, "I think you almost have to tell the person, right?"

"You can ask me," he said without looking up.

"I'm sorry?"

"You can ask me if I've told anyone about us."

"That's not wh—"

"Police work isn't only run-over-there, stop-that and break-it-up," he said. "They do teach us to read people. That is, if you don't have a talent for it to begin with."

"How was it for you?" I asked. "Talent or teaching?"

"No."

"That's not an answer."

"It is to the question you want to ask. No, I haven't told anyone I work with about us. Ready?"

He noticed the approaching waitress. Through her tired, moss-green eyes I wished I could see the two of us together at the table, to understand what a stranger thought of us. Ill-fitted? Intended? No, the woman likely paid us no attention, our orders taken with a bored, end-of-shift shrug. Beef stew for him. Ham sandwich for me.

"You're taking quite a chance," I said. "Someone could see us together. The Captain's daughter. Such a scandal."

He eased back, wrapping his bent arms around the top corners of the chair, hooking his thumbs in belt loops. "People know I spend time with your family. The Captain treats me like everyone else."

"That, I don't believe."

"What happened to politeness absolving dishonesty?"

I squinted down, the tip of my nose a blurry bud. With astonishing speed, the waitress returned. We shoveled into our meals.

"Not bad," he said. "Not as good as your mother's cooking."

"Mom's good. I'm not. Neither is Elizabeth. Tom doesn't seem to mind."

"Newlyweds can overlook deficiencies."

"Yes, such a deficiency, a woman who can't cook."

"You're the one who mentioned Tom."

"Fair enough." My tongue glossed over my front teeth. "He might mind later. And I bet something he doesn't like about her now might grow on him. It happens. The charming becomes bothersome and the bothersome becomes charming. You can see it with my parents."

"I don't."

"No? What happened to reading people?"

"Maybe I think too much of your parents to judge them. I do think a lot of them."

"Well, obviously."

This time, Orest knew enough to laugh. Hard and quick, like a bat hitting a ball. The vibration radiated through my body, as if I had risen in the morning solely for that reaction.

"You do laugh," I said.

"When someone says something humorous, yes."

He wove together flattery and insult with such ease. I remained quiet for a minute. I had spoken cautiously up until that point. Not quite myself.

"You can ask me, too," I said. "Working in a hospital isn't all file-this and process-that."

He pushed back from the table, slid to the end of his chair, leaned forward. His eyes around the restaurant. In the most honest tone I had yet to hear from him, he asked, "Well, why did you want to get married?"

I tossed my napkin on the table and threw back my neck: "Blahhhh."

"What?" He looked around apologetically at the other diners, as if to assure them nothing unseemly would follow.

"It's fine. You have a right to ask. To hell with the rest of them, though. Everyone has the same question. It makes me so angry."

"Angry?"

"I'm angry because I should just accept that I'm dying, but they need an answer. They need an answer why I wanted to get married. It's not fair." I adopted a chunky, hoarse amalgamation of Mom's and Dad's and Elizabeth's voices. "'Amanda will die soon. It's just what happens. It's the plan. Amanda wants to get married. Why? What's this about? What's the reason?' That's why I'm angry."

"The two don't seem related."

"Really? Why am I dying?"

"Excuse me?"

"Why am I dying?"

"Your father said leukemia."

"That's right. There's a name for it, so it's easy to understand. It's science. Medicine. An unhealthy number of white blood cells. Period. It's physical. There's their answer. They can let it end at that. But why? Why me? What's the answer? That, they can ignore. They don't need to know more. They just need me to be fine with it, so they can go on with their lives."

"I don't think they just want to go on with their lives."

"I know that. It's not the point."

"What is?"

"The point is this is physical, too. There's their answer. It is. I'm young. You're young. You walked right into my house. Attraction, Orest. I can't be attracted to you? A marriage driven by attraction. That's not enough of an answer? I couldn't be attracted to you? It has to be something strange, something unusual. I resent it."

"Don't resent me."

"I don't. Not yet."

"Not yet? Don't forget I married you."

"Because I'm dying." I mimicked his birthday-night performance, voice husky, complete with histrionic arm-shaking.

"I'm not laughing," he said.

"You should. It's funny. And true. I'm dying. You're honorable. You're guilty. You couldn't say no."

"Guilty?"

"Yes, you're guilty. That's why you agreed to marry me."

"Your father asked me."

"And you felt too guilty to say no. You said as much the other night."

Disgrace kept him from a debate.

"Guilt is a powerful ally, Orest."

He sat upright, looking toward the front door, away from me. His jaw tightened, as if a dentist had probed into sore, soft tissue in his mouth.

"To be fair, I put you in a terrible position. How could you say no? Dad's your superior at work. You might've thought turning him down would hurt your career. It wouldn't have, with Dad, but you might've had that concern. And let's not forget about the meals and the family. You might've thought you would lose all of it if you didn't agree. Quite manipulative of me, no?"

"I didn't think about it in those terms."

"Well, it was manipulative, even if I didn't see it at the time. Maybe I did. I don't know. Either way, I'm sorry. I want you to know that."

"I don't think you have anything to be sorry about."

"Well, human motivation is complex," I said. "You know that, with what you do. I've studied a lot—mostly medicine—and I've seen no single map for what drives people. It's context and perspective and experience, everything about a person in what-ever decision she makes next. It's unique, as much as I hate that word. Yet people give it up so easily. I see it at the hospital. A doctor tells them they're sick and it's like he stole all of the choices they ever made. It's all or nothing for them."

"For them? Not for you?"

"Exactly. Look, I'm sick. It's nothing I did. Nothing anyone did. It's the—"

"The white blood cells."

"Right, the white blood cells. I tried to get better. It didn't work. There's nothing that can be done. I can't control it. I could stay in my room for the next six months, never leave the bed. No one would say anything. Or I could—"

"Get married?"

"Or I could get married."

"But why that?"

"Why?" I slowly dragged my front teeth over my bottom lip, rested my right arm on the table, the side of my head on my knuckles. No form or art, only a rapid-fire dispersal. "Because Elizabeth got to move out and Catherine got the bigger room. Because I didn't feel like going to Europe. Because you were handsome."

"Were?"

I lowered my head a few smug degrees. "Your looks have been lost on me for months."

"Lost on me, too."

"Because everyone who has ever spent time with me had to. Family. School. Work. Because maybe I wanted to make people curious about why I did something. It's all of it. Or none of it. Does it matter? It doesn't matter when it comes to me, to what's wrong with me. There has to be a reason, except when there isn't one. Then … Then, you have to accept it. You do. We don't. That's hypocrisy. Well, the marriage has to be accepted."

I ended with a semi-dramatic flourish. The upcoming seconds forked toward surge or conclusion. His choice.

"Accepted," he said with a half-smile, an antidote to the intensity.

I exhaled the fumes of righteousness, a twinge of satisfaction in my midsection. Our meals finished, the bill paid, we stepped outside into a city in transition. The temperature had fallen. Backlighted by streetlamps and moon luster, people hurried around in search of trouble, as if it were in short supply. The walk home, speedy, no lagging. I still had more on my mind.

"What was it like when my father asked you?"

"I was polishing my shoes."

"That's what you remember?"

"That's what I remember. I wasn't expecting anyone. I was polishing my shoes for the next day. Someone came to the door. I thought it had to be Mrs. Sullivan with new towels. She was always bringing new towels. No one else had ever come to see me."

"Did he ask straight out or did he ramble? He rambles when he's nervous."

"He rambled. Wasn't himself, I could tell right away. Looked different. Sounded different. He wouldn't look at me. He kept staring at my bookshelves. They were empty, so there was nothing to see. He first said you were sick. I didn't know why he had come all that way to tell me. He finally got to the real reason."

"Surprised?"

"Surprised."

"Did you research leukemia before you said yes, just to make sure there wasn't a chance I'd get better?"

"No, but I probably should have. Everything happened quickly."

"Well, I'm not getting better, so you have nothing to worry about. How long did it take you to make up your mind?"

"I told him I needed the night. He said he understood. I could see he didn't."

"I would've thought you needed more than that."

"I actually needed less. I thought about him walking home. It was so cold outside that night. Maybe if it hadn't been so cold, I wouldn't have agreed. I thought about him going over what he would have to say to your mother and to you. An atrocious day for all of you already. No reason for me to make it any worse. I ran after him, found him on the street. Told him I would do it."

"See? I was right. Guilt."

"Sounds like a reasonable enough explanation."

About three blocks from the house at that point, I said, "You do know your reputation will soar, right?"

"My reputation?"

"Sure. People will know about this eventually. They'll say, 'There goes Orest Alworth. He granted that poor Bannon girl her dying wish.' You'll be a hero. And I'll be just that: the poor Bannon girl. As always."

Orest seemed to disappear into dead air and disquiet.

"What? That upsets you? That's how I'd be remembered if you married me or not. At least I got to be the first Mrs. Orest Alworth."

By a fraction-of-a-second, my stride slowed. He noticed. "Something else?" he asked.

I gnawed the right corner of my mouth. "Your name. Our marriage certificate says your first name isn't Orest or even Orestes. It's Michael. Michael O. Alworth."

"That's right."

"Why don't you go by Michael?"

"No one ever called me Michael growing up. It became Orest for some reason. It must've been what someone wanted."

A lie. Its detection noteworthy, I knew. Spouses spend entire marriages unable to notice bends in the truth, even outright deception. I immediately caught his lie. I would not challenge him, though. Too much already said in only a few hours. Almost too much.

"Catherine wanted us to use her middle name a few years ago," I said as we neared the house.

"What is it?"

"Veronica. She thought it sounded more mature. Didn't work. She gave up after a few days."

We had arrived. Orest unlocked the front door and let me through first. I went straight for the stairs, delaying for a moment, keeping my back to him. I risked the entire night with what I asked next: "Can I call you Michael?"

"No."

His answer, a bullet meant to warn, not pierce. Regardless, never again, I understood.

"We can have dinner together another night, just the two of us," he said, pitching up high his last words.

I paused on my way up to the second floor. "I would like that."

CHAPTER FIFTEEN

The Aunt

"What's my middle name?" he asked, that bratty, seven-year-old voice of his scraping my eardrums.

"You don't have one," I said. Slid my fingernail under the next page in the book, pushing it over, my eyes never on him. "I told you before."

"That's not true. Everyone has one."

I did not acknowledge him. My indifference usually tired him out, dispatched him to another activity, leaving me at peace. Not this day. His inquisitiveness, his intrusions, so maddening, just spikes beneath my skin, jabbing at my spine. Better when he was an infant. Crying better than questions. He grabbed my elbow.

"No! It's not true! Tell me!"

I threw the book to the side, the far pillow barely catching it before crashing into picture frames and vases. Anger pooled in my mouth and cheeks. Not only over this moment. Anger for all of them, every single irritating minute. He backed away, wiggling left to flee the room. I snared him, under his ribcage. My fingers vised into his triceps, shaking him for emphasis.

"I said you don't have one. Listen to me when I tell you something."

His eyes closed hard. Water dripped on his lashes. I tugged him by the wrist, over to the tall, dark-wood double doors. The never-enter room. His uncle's study, one place in the house he absolutely was not allowed. The hinge squeak, so loud, like church bells before a service. Always so cold inside, the air heavy with pipe smoke and whiskey. The sirens and mumbles between my husband and me, all the boy ever heard from outside. Neither of us ever happy when exiting. A place for the serious and the sad and the angry.

I flung him into one of the two leather chairs in front of the massive desk, that shiny monument of masculine power. He barely could see over it, around it. His legs dangled, not hitting the floor. He would not run away. Not then. I had struck him obedient, at last. Over to the large filing cabinet, I opened a drawer. Fingertips ran over the tabs, from front to back. Shut it. Opened another one. The tick of the big clock in the corner kept the rhythm of my breathing. Found it. Whipped the folder down on the desk, the puff of air shifting loose papers inches over.

"Here. Look at this."

Laid it out flat, sheets and cards of different sizes and shapes, packed together in no order. So sloppy. I took out one document. "This is your birth certificate. It's official. Came from the hospital when you were born. Read, right there." Pointed to his name.

His head skimmed left-to-right. No sound.

"Read it out loud," I said.

His mouth moved, only wheezy nothingness coming out. Finally, a piano hammer grazing the loosest wire: "Michael Alworth."

"Between it," I said. "What does it say between it? Read all of it."

"Michael O. Alworth."

"There. See?"

"It's an 'O.'" Confusion puckered his mouth. "What does it mean?"

"That's all it is. An 'O.' It doesn't mean anything. I told you this before."

"But why?"

"It's what your father wanted. Before you torture me with another why, I don't know the answer. You know as much as I do. The end of it. Understand?"

I leaned over him, put the birth certificate back in the folder. He slapped it down with both hands.

"No. I want to keep it."

"It's not yours to keep." Peeled off his fingers. Over to the drawer, the documents returned. "And you better not ever come looking for it. Your uncle never can find you in here."

Chair leather rumbled, his little frame squirmed. So defeated, he looked. Took his hand, took him from his seat, tenderly this time. "Maybe now you'll listen to me when I tell you something," I said, leading him out of the never-enter room. "Remember, I don't care enough to lie to you."

CHAPTER SIXTEEN

Amanda

Sickness poured from me. Coughs splattered bits of filth from my lungs on the walls, on the floor. Too loud. Pulled back my head and tried to muffle the gags and heaves. Involuntary. Everything had become so involuntary. I had spat out all of my self-control.

Unraveled on the bathroom floor, the tiles so cold against my skin. Each drop of sweat carved a long path from brow to ground. Too hot for June. Too hot. Expected the heat in July, August, but not then. I had waged a queasy battle all day. So many days like it since May. The worming discomfort. The lightning pain up the left side. Crunched and contorted to find whatever position would let me rest. Had no appetite. Fatigue, just present, all of the time.

That evening, something wicked and new inside me. Had to be the heat. The sun had chased all life indoors. The late afternoon, usually loud with neighborhood games and summertime activities, fell mute. The temperature seemed to have burned all sound from the city. The heat cooked whatever sat in me, boiling over near two in the morning, sending me into the bathroom. Tried to move silently. Just in time, I made it, my bones shaken by a beast.

More than ill, I felt alone. The sleeping city, a silent warehouse of toy houses. On those toss-and-turn nights when much younger, I imagined men, like my father, who worked in Newark's empty hours. Mom, right down the hall, made me feel safe. Even Elizabeth and Catherine in their beds, useless in any practical sense, gave me some security. Age had robbed me of those little-girl tricks. I felt alone. Alone, I hoped to remain right then.

The noise. I worried about the noise. I could not disturb Orest. The bathroom acoustics, with the tight, hard walls, amplified every sound. My gasps and hacks risked it all, everything from the previous weeks.

Close. I would not say we had become close. Perhaps not as removed, not as distant. Others might have ignored the signs. He sometimes pulled my chair out at the table. When he spoke with me during a meal, he used a lower volume. Not a whisper, but quiet enough so only I could hear. On walks home, we shared a few lines of conversation, like polite exchanges between strangers asking about a seat on a train or time on a watch.

"How was work?"

"Fine."

"Did you like dinner?"

"Yes."

Responses soon expanded with "very much." He dove into full dialogue with "You?"

At the front door, there were no more terse good-nights. No excuses of unmet responsibilities to bring the evening to a fast close. Our sentences continued from the street into the entryway. One night, he leaned against the banister at this easygoing angle, both hands in his pockets, elbows loose, motivated by nothing but finishing his thoughts. We sometimes talked as we made our way up the stairs to the second floor. Orest once even kept speaking—yelling, really—from inside his room as we each dressed for bed.

Certainly not romance. Maybe companionship, with its harmless implications. Perhaps too much. Whatever it was, I did not want it to end, so we had to stay in the house, the two of us together. Everything would stop otherwise. A race, the illness against my marriage.

It had to be the heat.

If not, I had fallen behind.

The time? Raised my head an inch or so from the floor. Ratcheted up by the smallest increments. Finally straight, I stuck my back to the wall for a few minutes. Threw my right arm across my chest and did some corkscrew motion to push myself upright. My head made it just above my waist. More sickness, more noise. And my greatest fear.

"Amanda," Orest said from outside the bathroom door.

My salivary glands exploded, panic drooling down my chin. I tried to ignore him.

"Amanda," he repeated, almost a shout. "Can I come in?"

"No."

"Should I get your mother?"

"No," I screamed, so beyond my character. He adopted the role of Officer Alworth. I became a cornered criminal without an escape.

"Amanda," he said, "either I come in there or I get your mother."

Either option, I hated.

"Come in," I said in defeat.

I braced for the quick, dramatic swoosh of the door. Instead, it crept slowly, shyly. Pre-dawn hallway darkness and dull bathroom light mixed to hide his face. Pity and disgust, I did not see, but felt. Felt them both.

"I'm sorry, Orest," I said, burying my head in my chest. "I'm sorry."

No reply. Just the running faucet. He wet a washcloth in the sink. Wrung out the excess drops and folded it lengthwise. Held the back of my neck with his right hand, pressed the cloth against my forehead, wiped it across my left cheek. I closed my eyes so hard I hoped I could blind us both from the image: tousled hair, stained gown, swollen skin splotched maroon and gray.

"What happened?" he asked.

"It was the heat."

A lie, he knew, but did not argue. Instead, he asked a question so intuitive in its construction.

"You don't want me to get your mother?"

Shook my head. "My mother would destroy everything," I could not tell him.

"Would you like to go to your room?"

"Yes, if I can. I had trouble before, but I—"

His right arm around my back, below my shoulders. His left arm under the bend in my knees. Shock ran through me. He picked me off the floor without much effort. Such a sensation, again involuntary. No control over myself. Wholly controlled by him. A breeze coated my ankles and feet. At the doorway, he turned to lead with my legs, sweeping me inside in one smooth motion. Lowered slowly into the bed, my fingers dug into his back. I wanted no separation, not from his warmth. Such an odd reaction to an incident started by heat. Looking up, I said, "Please don't tell my parents."

No answer. He left the room, left me to worry. So shriveled, I could not stop him. He returned with a blanket and pillow. Dropped them and himself to the floor, several feet away from the bed. Not a word. I sank deeper and deeper into the mattress, questions and fear wrapping around and around my face like gauze, cutting off my sight, blocking out my air.

Dryness. Dryness in my mouth woke me. Opened my eyelids with such deliberation, I doubted myself capable of mindless actions, like blinking. Immobilized. Every drop of moisture and nourishment drained from me, nothing to function. Trembling, my eye caught a dazzle from the nightstand, a formless crystal. My consciousness clawing out of sleep, my vision steadied. A glass filled with water reflected light from the window.

Orest?

Mom?

Up in a rush, my head throbbed. Rubbed the base of my hand hard against my left socket. Focus. The fear released adrenaline. No stirrings in the house, though. No signs of anyone else. Had he listened to me? Had he done his part? I had to get to my mother as soon as possible. Any delay would activate maternal instincts. The scare whipped me up and out of bed. A sight sucked my stomach tight against my ribs: Orest's blanket and pillow on the dresser. Why? Had he forgotten them? Never mind, not right then. Mom waited.

"How do you feel?" she asked when I arrived at the house.

"Fine. Just tired. So hot yesterday."

"It was hot. I didn't get much rest. Your father fell right to sleep. He can do that. I'm jealous."

That was it. No excessive flubbing on my part, trying to convince her only the ordinary had occurred the previous evening, theatrics that would have produced the exact opposite effect. Back in the bedroom that night, I heard Orest's rackety homecoming. He knocked on my door and entered after a few seconds. He stood as if he belonged there.

"Feeling better?"

"Yes, not as hot today. I'm sorry about last night."

"No apologies necessary."

"Thank you, then. More than you should've been asked to do," itself the cousin of an apology.

He said nothing.

"Thank you," I said, spluttering slightly, "for not telling anyone. I hope you understand, I just—"

"If you don't mind, Amanda," he interrupted, the words like gravel locked in his mouth, "I think I should stay here again tonight. If you don't mind."

"It's not necessary."

"Maybe not, but you needed help and you wouldn't ask for it. You won't let me tell your parents. You're leaving it to me to take care of you."

"Honestly, Orest, it was just that one night." I argued for a result I did not really desire.

"Either I stay in here or I tell your parents."

I nodded. He ducked away. An excitement—one thought lost—through my hands, down to my fingertips, up my arms, into my chest. I would have a night in the same room with Orest. Not like the prior one, clouded by illness, with only pain and drowsiness. The prospect of his company pulsed through me and with it, a vibe of immortality.

He returned and kept the door open. Blanket out and down, a crisp drop into a crouch, hands planted on the floor, legs springing from underneath him. Such professionalism, his exact motions declaring: *I'm here for one reason and one reason only.* The purely mechanical nature gave no room for comment. I still had to make one.

"It must be uncomfortable on the floor."

"I've had worse," he said, turning on his left side, away from me.

No words followed.

CHAPTER SEVENTEEN

Orest

The next evening, back to her bedroom, back on the floor. The following night, too. After a week, we both accepted it, expected it, without any discussion. We did not talk much. If we did, nothing meaningful. "How was your day?" "How do you feel?" I filled the role of watchman, like in the army, when we each had to take our turn in a rotation. Except no one else to rotate with in Amanda's room.

Late one night, she again became sick. Flat on my stomach on the ground, I heard her twist and toss. She struggled out of bed, almost tripping over my ankles on her way to the bathroom.

"Amanda?" I said outside the door after a few minutes.

"I'm fine. Really." Firm, convincing. "I'll be out soon."

The faucet spritzed on for several seconds. The door opened. She looked not quite as ill as the other evening. Still not well, though. That she let me see her in this state seemed to mark progress, in some odd way.

"Was it the heat?" I asked.

"Of course," she said, dry and sharp. "It always is."

With my right arm around her back, just under her shoulders, I guided her to the bedroom. She probably did not need the assistance, but I could not let her walk by herself.

"I'm afraid it'll be getting worse," she said. "My side feels like it's on fire. That's my liver and spleen. I'm so tired. Lying down is uncomfortable, though. Getting bruises all over my arms and legs. None of this is good. All expected."

"You sound like a doctor."

"That was the plan."

I did not respond. Not what she wanted. Doubt I ever responded how she wanted.

"Surprised?" she asked.

"No, I—"

"I'm used to it." Her thighs shook as she lowered herself on the bed. "When I told the sisters at Saint Vincent's, they said I should become a nun."

"I could see that."

"Charming." Seated, air fast into her lungs, each word coughed more than spoken. "Took a bad turn right before graduation. My parents wouldn't let me go to college right away. We had a deal. Work for two years, then see how I felt."

"Where?" I sat on the floor, my arms, tentpoles staked behind me.

"The hospital," she said, her upper lip curled, her eyes wide with hurt.

"I know where you worked. Where for college?"

"Right." Her mouth relaxed. "New Jersey College for Women in New Brunswick. Don't exactly know where my parents would let me go. Probably wherever was closest. After that, Woman's Medical College in Philadelphia."

"Philadelphia?"

"I did have ambitions beyond the city limits of Newark." She flattened herself out on the bed, a long huff out through her nose. "To think, I gave it all up to marry you. Would have started this fall. This isn't how I thought it would turn out."

"That makes one of us."

She and I laughed at the same time, for the first time. I suppose we could have called it a start. To what, I did not know. Conversation continued almost every night. Not like the other conversations I had during the day. Those were about work or the other officers' families. None of them knew much about me. And I cannot remember too many people ever wanting to know much about me the way Amanda did. I suppose I mostly spoke with men and men rarely care about details. She and I eventually moved beyond questions about moods and comments from the family and ordinary events.

"It's boring," she said one night when I asked about growing up with sisters.

"Just tell me."

"But I don't tell stories well. It's a limitation. I never did well in literature. I mean, well enough. I can remember things I read very well, almost photographically.

But telling you what so-and-so author meant, that's not for me. Believe it or not, that's Elizabeth. Literature was her best subject."

"You're about to lose me," I said, on my back, arms above my shoulders, head in interlocked fingers.

"Fine. It's about the Coast. Dad would be so angry if he knew we even thought of going there. He always forbade us. Made it much more tempting. Elizabeth had to go. The two of them would argue about it. This was a few years ago, before she met Tom. Well, one night, she told my parents she would be out with some friends. She told me to say I was coming here, to see Aunt Cecilia. And we did. She was with friends for a little. I was here for a while. That way, if anyone asked them, they wouldn't be lying."

"Clever," he said.

"Risky and reckless, more like it. Anyone could have seen us. An officer. A neighbor. Could have told my father. I was almost sick. Elizabeth was so defiant. Just so confident. I mean, she always had poise, but that night, something else. We stepped right into one of the clubs. She didn't hesitate. We took a table in the back. No one noticed us. Everyone was too busy trying to be seen or trying not to be seen. We stayed for two songs. I can't tell you the names. I'd probably remember if I heard them. We walked out and ran home."

"No one ever found out?"

"No one ever found out. My mother might have suspected something. As long as we were safe, she was happy Elizabeth and I did something together. I guess it was nice growing up here," she said. "Not so bad, looking back. But why did you ever come to this place? You could have gone anywhere, right?"

"Almost. The job. Something new," I said.

"Did you decide to join the police because of your father?"

"Maybe. Maybe not. I liked the army. Not all of it, but the structure. Police work seemed enough like the army that I thought it might suit me. The fact my father was on the force confirmed it for me, I guess. So, yes, he probably had something to do with it."

"Interesting, isn't it, how we can become our parents without even trying? Even when we're trying not to be them."

"Don't quite follow," I said.

"Well, look at me. I promised myself I never would become my mother."

"I like your mother."

"I do, too. But you can like someone without wanting to become the person. I was going to be a doctor, about the farthest I could imagine getting from her. But what am I now? A police officer's wife living on Pennsylvania Avenue. Between Elizabeth and Catherine, I was the least like Mom. Now, I'm more like her than they'll ever be."

"Not exactly," I said to her. "But even so, not so bad."

Amanda told better stories than I did, even if she didn't think so. I strung together facts without much elaboration. No mention of schools or friends or favorite games as a child, because no one else had ever asked. My stories, police reports: items in neat rows, written on invisible straight lines in my head. The truth occasionally jutted out, I admit. When it did, Amanda caught it. She listened as much to what I didn't say as to what I did. She would have made a good detective.

One story from my first days on the force: a criminal, a weapon, a pursuit and a confrontation. She asked a few questions that scraped against the surface, some humor trickling out. The perpetrator, inebriated and harmless. The gun, fake.

"How harrowing," she said.

"Not that one, maybe," I defended myself, "but I've been in dangerous spots."

"Really?" she said, turning over on her side, her arm and leg hanging off the bed. "Have you ever killed anyone?"

"Yes," I said, rolling away from her.

Not the job, not that she would have known.

"I'm sorry. I didn't mean to be so cavalier. I got carried away."

"You shouldn't be sorry. You're not to blame."

"Blame, blahhh," a geyser of air against the back of her throat.

"What?"

"Blame is such lazy word. Even the way it comes out of your mouth is lazy. Bl-ahhh. I blame someone for something that happened. I blame someone for something that didn't happen. Someone blames me."

"I'm blaming myself," I said, "not anyone else."

She was prepared. "That's just as bad."

"It's responsible."

"That's what people tell themselves. All has to be me, my fault. I don't know what you would call it, but it's as bad as blame."

"You don't know what you're talking about."

"He says to his dying wife. Call it an accident. Blame doesn't let you go. And for what? What do you get? It's useless."

A draft of silence blew into the room. She was not finished, though. She never really was ever finished.

"From what I've seen at the hospital, everything ends the same way, after the accidents and the illnesses. Once people reach that point, that point where they're not coming back, it almost doesn't matter how they got there."

"Sounds heartless," I said.

"It's not a moral judgment. It's science. At least mostly science."

"Mostly?"

"Early on, I asked Doctor Caputo how he knew someone was dying. They would run tests and track vitals, but the doctors seemed to understand when it was over before all of that, almost like an instinct. I'll never forget what he said: the absence of wanting. That's when you know someone is dying. A stomach stops wanting food. Lungs stop wanting air. A heart stops wanting to beat. Doesn't matter what brought a person to that moment. And, yes, there's biology and physiology behind it, with cells failing to replicate and such, but it goes beyond science at some stage. The body just stops wanting, almost on command. That's it. Death is the absence of wanting."

I did not respond.

"Are you still awake?" she asked

"Maybe. What about wanting the absent? Can't that be too much?"

"Maybe. Probably," she said. "Sounds more philosophical than medical. You'll have to ask someone else."

In the darkness, rest seemed to drape over both of us at once, like a giant sheet, not unlike in the barracks with the other soldiers years ago. From underneath, I said out loud, when I easily could have kept it to myself: "The absence of wanting. Wanting the absent. Either could kill a person."

CHAPTER EIGHTEEN

Amanda

As I had sketched out, the illness advanced. Weakness and retching. July burned in my skull. My dresses, looser each time I wore them. Mass and tissue melted off my bones. A critical phase, then an end. That would be the progression. Seen it so many times and when I did, I wondered how I would react when my turn arrived. I would be prepared, I had promised myself. My death, different. What everyone would remember about me, if anything at all. A peculiar girl who met a sad end.

When I had thought about the end, in the past, I did not anticipate having something to lose.

I would lose the routine. Routine, the death knell for some, a wily enemy resisted, fought and almost never defeated. But I adored our routine. The tea-before-bed, ten-pages-of-reading, lights-out routines probably took couples years to perfect. Orest and I had adopted a pattern so quickly, which gave me something close to pride. Perhaps even hope.

"Orest, it's time," I would say, the darkness of the bedroom gumming my throat. I would stumble past him, into the bathroom. In the hall, he waited, more alert on some occasions than others. We would snail back, his body a shadow directly behind mine, his right forearm extended in front, my hand fastened on. If I lost my balance, his left arm would swoop around my waist. Yes, a few times, I might not have been as unsteady as I let him think. I would sit on the bed, chest practically to knees, folded in half. His hand stayed on my back. After a few seconds, I would bow my head. Ready. Holding me in a compressed, crescent package, he would place me on my side and pull the blanket over me. Our routine.

One evening, one of my worst, having taken more minutes than usual to recover, I asked with bile still fresh in my mouth: "Is now the time to consummate the thing?"

He laughed. Loud at first, uncontrolled and honest. He trailed off. A few more laughs. More than necessary. A bit contrived, really. An exaggerated pause. Some sounds resembling laugher, like from a bumbling, amateur actor.

Too far.

"I wasn't serious, Orest," I said casually, trying to station myself on the right side of the joke. "Was just being funny."

"I know," he said, shaky, unconvincing.

"I wouldn't want to make you uncomfortable," I continued, ground and authority crumbling beneath me.

"You didn't." He turned over, away from me. "It's fine."

"People think what they think. Elizabeth. Tom. My mother, even. Catherine's too young. Not my father. Never would cross his mind. They shouldn't care. It's private, right? Whatever happens, whatever doesn't happen, it's no matter to them. We are married. If we wanted to, it would be fine. If we didn't, that's fine, too. No one should care, if we did or we didn't."

A dog barked twice in the distance. A garbage can rustled down the street. I clutched my bedspread up to my chin, already too warm. Too much. I had said too much. Asleep? Maybe he was asleep. The next words had to be his or there would be no words between us ever again.

"It's not that you're unattractive," he said.

"Tonight I am," a cheerful hammer against a disfigured nail.

"It's just," he hesitated, "it's just that you're sick."

"I know," I agreed, confident, dismissive, phony. "I know that. I feel better sometimes. Most mornings. Even some nights. Early, though. When we first get home from dinner—" I faded out, wanting him to finish the thought. An observation? An invitation? He had to decide. I did not know, myself.

No more talk between us, only suffocating, sticking-to-the-sheets embarrassment. How high could a temperature rise aided by humiliation? If alone, my fists would have pounded repeatedly into the mattress. A scream, not from the throat, but from much deeper inside me. The cry of a defeated barbarian. Instead,

I bottled it up, a lid shut tight on a boiling pot. Kept the covers on. Too exposed without them, even with no one to see. Someone would see, I feared. Someone had to see. Everyone who looked at me would know. Those who passed me on the street. My family. The humbling would glimmer off my face in a high-forehead shine.

He would see. The indignity burned enough in the dark. In daylight, incineration. Even he—dense, remote—could dredge up the sham kindness, the awkward-grin, no-problem-here façade that would make it all so much more unbearable. God, how awful. Could not happen. Off the bed and into the bathroom. Blanket around my shoulders, I sat in the corner, my back against the wall. Only a few hours. Safe until then. The sun eventually poked under the curtain, knocking me from half-sleep. Orest would wake soon and notice my absence. He would worry at first. Relieved? Maybe. Probably.

The doorknob twittered left-to-right. "Amanda," he said in a grainy, dawn octave.

"I'm in here. I'm fine," I said, clear and strong. "Use downstairs, please. I will be out later, after you're gone, probably."

He obeyed. Definitely a relief to him. Long an audience to his daily preparations, I listened. So much different from inside the bathroom than in the bedroom, the shoes-to-stairs, door-shutting finale as loud as a stampede. I waited a few minutes. He could return, having forgotten something. Had to be certain. With enough time gone, I pulled myself up, over to the sink, the mirror. My skin, dried-out putty. My eyes, rain-soaked stones held up by perpetual circles. No wonder.

"You don't look well," Mom told me over lunch that afternoon.

"I don't feel well," I said, an unimaginable answer. I would have spun a thousand excuses before an admission of decline. Not then. The truth, so much worse.

"Is it time, do you think, to start staying here?"

"Maybe." Again, unimaginable. "Not yet. I'm going to lie down." At least I had set Mom along a distracting trail. "Amanda's not feeling well," she would caution everyone. No questions. A diversion to let me wallow through the hours. Part anger. Part self-reproach. Confusion, as well. Perhaps I had bulldozed so many conventions, I no longer could recognize decency and prudence. I brought indignation back to Aunt Cecilia's house, tucking it with me under the blanket in bed. The first discussion after an incident always is about the incident, even if it receives no mention. If I delayed long enough, could we begin again, the memory expired? How long would it take? Start with one evening.

When Orest returned home, I shut my eyes and settled into the perfect fake-sleep position, like I had when Mom and Dad would check on me as a child. I worried I would be too stiff, too tight to convince him. Orest's expert people-reading would see through my nonsense. And he would think I lacked sophistication, the type of sophistication one requires for whatever

I had suggested the night before. Abandon the plan? Too late. I sensed him at the door.

"Amanda," he whispered, so low, he had no real intention to speak with me.

I did not answer. Away he went, perhaps not to return that night. But he did, a few minutes later, onto the floor. I remained so still, more so than if actually unconscious. Too stiff, too tight. It worked, though. An hour? Probably less. Asleep? Had he fallen asleep so easily? How could he, after everything? So callous. Not worthy of the offer. An offer? Was it even that? Not really. Only a comment. Definitely asleep. How could he? Damn him. I fussed aggressively, hitting the pillow. He did not stir. I huffed heavy air. Damn him.

"You look better," Mom told me the next day.

"I feel better," I said, sharp and fast. I let Orest walk out again that morning without a word, without a look.

"Any chance you want—"

"No, Mom. I told you not yet." Not the subject of the hostility, my mother, but a near-enough object. The release, I enjoyed, even if a bit guilty.

All day, the how-dare-he soliloquy circled in my head, gaining strength with each lap. I felt more certain as the hours passed. His mistake. His misinterpretation. His ego. I would punish him again that night. I would not acknowledge his feeble "Amanda" from the doorway, his return to the ground.

No. I would acknowledge him. More than that. I would talk to him. More like give him a talking-to, to borrow a phrase from Aunt Cecilia. I had performed well during debates in high school. In front of the class, notes on some paper, an inept adversary hawking a bland thesis. I always could retort and counter. The tactics, roughly similar for Orest. Arranged in my mind the flow of ideas, from point-to-point. By late afternoon, hours already sunk in strategy, I could not remember how it even became a debate. The consequence likely rested solely with me. Did I only want the chance to correct a misunderstanding, explain myself?

Boggled in my head, all the reasons, the purpose behind it, as I waited for Orest in the bedroom. Indifference. I had landed on indifference. Steady indifference would guide me. I sat up, arms ringed around my knees. Soon. He would arrive soon. But no sign of him at the expected hour. *Thirty more minutes, then worry*, I told myself. Ninety minutes after that, terror. I tore in a zigzag around the room. Thousands of these nagging nights, Mom must have had. Those always had worked out.

Downstairs. The irrationalizations one makes: *Wait downstairs and he will be safer.* So silly. So childish. Regardless, I went. Sat in a chair by the entryway. Maybe he would have informed me about his delay, if I had given him the opportunity. But no. If disaster had struck, Dad would have come over right away, right? Or another officer with bad news, the worst news? Finally, the jitter of his key and the suck-snap opening of a door swollen by summer air.

"What are you doing up?" he asked quietly, as if he would wake someone else.

"I was worried." My indifference, gone.

"Sorry, I didn't—"

"You don't have to whisper."

More loudly. "I said I didn't expect to be this late. We have a trolley strike. I was going to tell you, but … I didn't have the chance."

"It's fine. I couldn't sleep. Too hot up in the room. I thought I would come down here and read a little."

He looked around. No sign of a book.

"The heat's not making you sick, is it?"

"No, not today. I've been feeling not too bad the past few days."

The past few days? Why did I mention them, tie them together as a unit? They suddenly became an epoch, defined by a blundering inception and whatever went on between us at that moment, its potential conclusion. All of it, he seemed just as happy to bypass. I immediately put us back on the track of nonconfrontation, walking by him, starting up the stairs, asking in an upbeat style, "Trolley strike?"

"Yes, trolley strike," he followed me, tension dropping behind him with each step. "Has to end soon. We've been pulling multiple shifts, trying to make sure nothing gets too out of hand. We're all exhausted."

In the hallway, all so normal. We had cleared the wreck in one leap. I had my answer. With a bit of out-of-the-ordinary excitement, people can return to the "before" period, the unseemly forgotten, overlooked, swept away. Some nightly preparations and we took our places in the bedroom, in the dark, relaxed. We spoke with one another, detachment such a yesterday trick.

"I thought you might have widowed me," I said. "Wouldn't that be funny?"

"Not for me."

"Well, not funny, but a twist. You work in a dangerous profession. Could happen. The Widow Alworth. Wouldn't that be something? 'At least he had Amanda to make his last days so happy,' they would say."

"They would?"

"Of course. People would encourage me to marry again, to get on with my life, but I would resist, out of respect for you."

"Thank you."

A tempting pause. End there. I knew I should have ended there. But I could not help myself.

"You shouldn't, though."

"Shouldn't what?"

"Resist getting married again."

The easiness between us, vaporized in a few seconds. The room teetered. He gave a calm, professional plea: "Amanda, please don't do this."

"Do what?" I said with caricatured innocence. "What don't you want me to do?"

"Talk about it."

"What?"

"You know what I mean."

"No, I don't." Aimed at the ceiling, I neared eruption. "What don't you want me to talk about? You don't want me to talk about what it will be like when I'm gone? Is that it? I wouldn't want to upset you, Orest. Of course not. It must be so uncomfortable to think about what your life will be like a year from now, two years from now. That must be so uncomfortable. Let me stop. And your next wife. I won't talk about her either. Don't worry. Even though I want you to be happy, right? That's what everyone expects. That I want you to be happy. Not even notice I'm not here. Move on. That's what I'm supposed to want. That's what's expected, so that's what I'll do."

The ground settled, followed by an aftershock: "I wonder if we would have gotten along, your next wife and me."

"Stop it," he shouted.

"No," I sprang up, my hands dug under the top mattress, my torso perched over him. "You don't get to tell me to stop it. You don't. It's too hard for you? Too bad. You know what? Hear this: I hate her. I hate your wife. I hate her so much, Orest, because she gets everything. Is that too much for you? I hate her, Orest. It's the truth. I hate her so much."

I held for several seconds, my chest about to split open, my heart and lungs about to spray all over the floor. My tongue lapped fast over my mouth. Nothing from him. I tumbled back into the bed, depleted.

A minute or so gone, he responded gently, obliquely: "A lonely life is a hard trial for women."

"What the hell is that supposed to mean?"

"You're the one who knows about Aeschylus."

"What does that mean?"

"Amanda," he said, unmovable, so far beyond negotiation. "Trolley strike. I'm tired. You've talked. I listened. No more tonight."

He curled away from me. I felt only the cold perspiration above my lip, behind my knee bends.

CHAPTER NINETEEN

Amanda

Here lies Amanda, a seemingly reasonable young woman who behaved so erratically in the final months of her short life, she erased the pleasant image those who knew her might have cherished.

Too long for an epitaph? It fit. If not in typeset, definitely in tone. My imagination always baked hot in that transition space between being asleep and being alert. My first-morning ideas, if not the most lasting, the most interesting. I always intended to keep some paper next to the bed to write them down. Ralph Waldo Emerson did, I remembered reading. At least, I think he did. I might have made it up.

He already had gone that morning. Orest, not Emerson. Did not hear him. My senses frizzed like a broken-down appliance. He left behind his blanket and pillow, along with the buzz of that line: "A lonely life is a hard trial for women." What the hell did he mean? Honestly? A crafty way to end the conversation? A message? Some sort of riddle?

"You're the one who knows about Aeschylus."

Arms locked in a circle above my head, my ribs a relief map through stretched-out skin, I scrutinized the sentence from every angle, as if a mobile above me, rotating, revolving.

Familiar. Was it familiar? Too poetic, so it must have been Aeschylus. To Orest, language often seemed an irritating necessity of functional society. A faraway memory bell dinged. Did I know it? Perhaps. Projection? Like a despairingly sought umbrella imagined in room after room, spot after spot. I could insert the quotation into all sorts of works. One possibility broke from the pack, running out in front, the others lagging behind. Up from the bed.

"You're early," Mom greeted me in the kitchen.

"Catherine hasn't left yet, has she?"

"When has she ever left early for school? She's in her room."

Up the stairs fast, almost fearful my sister could have escaped through a secret hatch that did not exist. At her bedroom, five rapid knocks.

"I'll be down in a minute," Catherine said, yanking open the door. "Amanda?"

I gave a fast glance around the room. Neater than usual.

"I need a favor." Handed her a piece of paper. "I need this book. They should have it in the library at school. They did when I was there."

"Why this?"

"It's just something I have to see. It's important to me. You can't tell anyone. Please. No comments at dinner or mentioning it to Dad or anything like that. This is between us. Catherine, I understand you're angry with me, but I probably won't ask you for anything—"

"Stop," she said, her arms thrown up. "I'm not a child."

She was correct, I recognized then. Not a child, but also not an adult. An adult casts a grudge in marble, each day polishing up that masterpiece of self-involvement. A child can let ill feelings disintegrate in mere hours. And Catherine had let hers do just that. She still wished for me to believe some bitterness remained, for emotional leverage, for mystery. Yet as she left for Saint Vincent's, I knew I had appointed the perfect emissary: enough of an adult for discretion, enough of a child for devotion, enough of an adolescent for slinking self-possession.

Let it be right, I thought to myself over the morning hours, waiting in my old bedroom, as if sentenced there by doubt. If not right, then a day lost. Could be no other possibility. None at all. Unless there were. No, I was certain, although my certainty did not guarantee accuracy. Even when wrong, so insistent, so stubborn. More at stake now than intellectual pride.

Not even eleven. The day had not even reached eleven, yet my mind spit and stuttered as if dragged around by a berserk animal. Obsession had returned. The sickness should have corroded and disabled those synapses that conducted my obsession, like rust and plaque on a decrepit textile mill. But no. So much already lost, why not the obsession? Such a cruel trick. Interruption. I had to have an interruption to save me. Deliverance from an unlikely source: Elizabeth. As if summoned by my subconscious yammering, she appeared before me and said, "Let's go out. Let's take a walk."

So odd, of course. Unprecedented really, with no reason offered as to why she had shown up at that moment. I usually would have distrusted her. Torn away the wrapping to expose the bare motivation. Not then. I appreciated the interference. I closed behind me the bedroom door. Jostled the handle, making sure it stayed shut. I had to trap my worry in that one space, where it would wait for me later in the day.

Once outside, the sun beamed into strange places—up through my nose, behind my ears, into the slim rings of my eye sockets—as if cleaning out an infection. I felt like a shiny piece of a broken glass bottle, light thrown off from a speck, blinding anyone within several feet. The blindness, I did not mind. I did not wish to be seen, to be known.

"I thought we would go to Lincoln Park," Elizabeth said.

The suggestion, too premeditated. Struck me as suspicious. No longer my savior, she might have exposed herself as an envoy dispatched by the family. Perhaps Orest had alerted everyone that his wife—their daughter, their sister—had severed her final tie with sanity. I would be led to an open area—a park with lunching businessmen and mothers with babies in carriages—where I would not cause a disturbance when dealt unfortunate news. Perhaps at the same time, my parents would move my belongings from Aunt Cecilia's house. As we took our seats on a bench, I lanced right through the pleasantries.

"What does Mom want to know?"

"What? Why would you say that?" Elizabeth's shriek cut through years of postured maturity, her eldest-child superiority landing in shreds on the grass of Lincoln Park. A few heads turned in our direction. A disturbance, in fact, could follow, I saw, but not of my making.

"Something happened," I said, both question and statement.

"No, not today. But, yes, something. It's good. Should be. I don't want to tell Mom or Tom just yet. Certainly not Dad. I just need to say it all out loud first, to talk with someone. Someone who won't judge me right away."

"Ha," I blurted into the wind. "Judgment is the basis of our relationship."

"Don't say such a thing. It's not only that." Such earnestness from her, so beyond the norm.

I waited a few moments, looking toward the sleek, alabaster columns of the Dryden Mansion, wondering what concerns bounced around its walls. A little while longer, I asked, "What is it then?"

"I'm going to have a baby," she said so quietly, as if even a touch more volume would have ricocheted the news around the city.

I could feel springs and gears moving inside me, like a winding watch. Jealousy? Perhaps. Sadness? Perhaps. Happiness, as well. I immediately could feel a vicarious existence beyond that instant. Yes, within me, a primal burst, a celebration over the continuation of our species of Bannons.

"That does sound good, no?" Purposely included the last word to undercut the judgment she feared.

Elizabeth's head floated in an indeterminate shape of yes-and-no.

"You haven't told Tom?"

"No, I only saw the doctor two days ago. I wanted to let Tom know right away. But when I walked home from the appointment, I ran an errand in one store. I stopped in another. Then, another. I was stalling and I didn't know why. I convinced myself I was so tired when I got home that I should wait to give him the news after I had rested. The next day, I couldn't do it. Couldn't say it out loud. Once I did, it would become real and I don't know if I'm ready for it to be real. I can't take back the first reaction he'll see. If I don't seem happy enough, he'll always wonder."

I stayed quiet, too quiet for Elizabeth, who asked, "Do you think I'm terrible?"

"No, of course not. Not being honest with yourself, that would be terrible."

"But it's what I should want, right?"

"I think *should* is a lie everyone seems committed to keep telling."

With an it-figures gag in her throat, Elizabeth did not hold back her snitty eye-roll and prideful stare in the opposite direction. "That's not what I need."

I became angry. More of the same from her. More selfishness and conceit. Searching for assurance and confirmation, not honesty. To have come to her dying sister with the "problem" of a child, a real marriage and ongoing prospects. Such arrogance. Such insensitivity.

"I don't know what you need me to tell you," I said. "That there's nothing wrong with how you feel? That you'll be a good mother? That everything will be fine?"

Elizabeth strained her eyes shut, her lids so tight, the pain seemed to leak through the cracks. And I understood I was wrong. Not more of the same. This was her apology, her apology for everything. For childhood slights and know-it-all decrees. For living beyond the next year and for having a baby. Elizabeth had approached me with an offering: a truth she would share with me and no one else. What she believed worst in herself, her husband never would know, just as no one other than my sisters ever would know what I considered worst in myself. A strong current blew my hair in wild directions. The overhead sun exposed the marks and blots and lines I hated about my face. The same effect for Elizabeth. We sat in our own imperfections, as we would with no one else, the imperfections we each would allow only the other to see. I was known by my sister, if not anyone else. What a comfort, I realized, to be known by someone, both the good and the bad.

"The answer is yes to all of them," I said. "Nothing is wrong with how you feel. You'll be a good mother. Everything will be fine. At least, I think it will. You don't give yourself enough credit. And you don't give Tom enough credit. Maybe you'll be happy as a mother. Maybe you won't. What do any of us know? You'll make it work, regardless. That I know."

Saccharine and a bit trite, but what Elizabeth needed.

"Thank you," she said, the gratitude reaching into our past, as well as across the future, to those days in years to come when she would remember me with nothing but fondness. "I'll tell him tonight."

We walked back to the house, leaving behind in Lincoln Park both incompletion and finality. If we could have read one another's thoughts, I would have seen Elizabeth's disappointment over our not having put to rest sooner those issues neither of us could quite identify, permitting us to enjoy a bit longer the adult phase of sibling confidence. She would have glimpsed my gratitude for her resisting any end-of-days wailing. Instead, she had given me something rather ordinary, letting live a little while longer the possibility the two of us could have more talks, perhaps several more.

For the rest of the afternoon, I remained in bed. Tried the windowsill, but my bones were too exposed. No cushion for my back against the wood. I waited for Catherine's return, usually accompanied by trumpets of teenage boisterousness: doors swung and slammed, cries of "I'm home!" Not then. Around three, she slipped into the room so carefully, she startled me.

"Here it is. It's the only copy. You can have it for four days."

I took the book, sat up crossed-legged and began studying. A younger version of Catherine would have loitered, pried. She left. The door shut. No questions asked.

The Oresteia of Aeschylus, translation by Lewis Campbell. Maybe not the one I had read in school, but it would do. Pages snapped and sliced with each fast turn, the mildew-library scent puffing against my face. Line after line mingled together, none of the meaning sinking in. Not necessary. I would focus on one word: *lonely*. It would stick out. Had to find it.

I did.

On page ninety-four, Clytemnestra to Orestes: "A lonely life is a hard trial for women."

First, the problem-solved tingle of satisfaction through my back, as if I had earned a high mark on a test. As the last spark crackled off my top vertebra, my stare went cloudy around the borders. The off-white page glowed, backlighting the gray-black font. Tension trekked to my heart. He knew. He knew everything. The story, his story: the son who kills the mother who killed his father. Shuffle the sequence, swap chance for revenge, the impact, equally brutal. He more than knew. Branded it in his memory. A memory seemingly so uncluttered, yet packed with these vicious words. Not that sentence alone. All of them, lodged in his head:

"You were my parent, and then recklessly exposed me to misfortune."

"I am full of pain for what is done and suffered and for our whole race."

"But how shall I escape my father's Furies, if I neglect this act?"

Repeated and repeated and repeated, the running monologue. Furies. Misfortune. Pain. Background noise at first. Impossible to shut off, to quiet. Sound becoming more than sound. A voice. Unchallenged. Uninterrupted. Molding. Directing. All he could hear. *Tick, tick, tick,* his mind's clock racing.

Not all of him in those lines, on those pages, I knew. More than that. Enough of him, though. Why those words then? I lingered on the scene: a woman ranting before her death. Would he dare? A comparison? An assault? Not fair. Not fair at all. My throat tight, a furious scrunch plumping the skin between my eyes, above my nose. Every female with a point of view, a legitimate grievance, easily packaged as the villain, the murderess? More to talk about that night. Perhaps all of it. Nothing off limits. I resumed my rehearsal from the day before. A different script, but the same intent, the same audience. That he could mean this about me—

Or none of this at all.

I read more. More context. Furies. Misfortune. Pain. Sympathy? A sympathetic figure? Was I to him? Not pitiable, but sympathetic. Was he to me? In truth, between us, perhaps not sympathy, but empathy, as echoed in his blunt, unspoken retort: *Listen to what I know, what I live with. My story, as sad and tragic and lonely as yours.*

Assault or empathy? Which to accept, to believe? Which?

"Amanda," I heard Catherine say softly. My eyes opened from a quick doze, unplanned and undesired. "It's time for dinner. Everyone's downstairs."

"I'll be there in a minute." I flopped my hand around the bed, reaching for the book. "You can take it back."

Before stepping out, Catherine said, "Orest is here."

A deep breath blown out through round cheeks. Assault or empathy? Which? Out of the bed, down the stairs, into such a typical scene: the family herding by the entrance of the dining room, all agreeable. Orest gave me a look: his brow up fast, eyes big, lips sealed hard. He pulled out my chair at the table and sat next to me. A normal meal, not an aftermath. When the evening concluded, we exited for an interminable journey of several yards down the sidewalk. Where had we concluded? Where to begin?

"How's the strike?" I asked.

"Over, thank God."

"Yes, thank God." All so superficial. Would everything be from that point? Into the house and about our pre-bedtime business. Neither of us suggested any break from the routine. Orest took the floor. I took the bed.

Assault or empathy?

I chose empathy.

"Orest, I need to apologize."

"No, you don't."

"Yes. Yes, I do." Wished I could end there, tarp everything with one apology, with no reason to inventory the offenses, whatever they might have been. Not enough, I knew. I had to say more.

"Why don't we just call it an accident?" he said.

"Christ!" Slapped both hands to my face, covering my eyes. "Do I sound that obnoxious?" I groaned between my palms, the sound amplified, modulated.

A pant of air through his nose, almost a laugh. "Not the word I would use."

"Really, though? It's obnoxious, hearing how I sound. I put clever words together in a clever way. I come up with these phrases and sayings and opinions, just to make me seem—I don't know—wise, interesting. Blame. Choice."

"Guilt," he joined in.

"Yes. See?" Leaned on my side to look at him. "It's ridiculous. I think they mean something. Package it all into these little sayings and I expect them to mean something. But then I have a spectacle like last night. Where were they then? Gone. They mean nothing and I sound so, I don't know, immature, silly for even having said them."

I flung myself flat on the bed.

"I think you're being too hard on yourself," he said.

"Maybe. Maybe we're all too hard on ourselves. I think that's what I want to tell you. Not that I'm sorry. I don't want to be a reason for you to be hard on yourself."

"That sounds like another clever saying," he said, antagonizing me, playfully so.

"Stop. I've said a lot of things. Said some awful things last night." A pause. "And I meant them. I meant them all. I can't tell you I didn't. It was the truth." I again turned on my side, facing him. "That's what I hope you hear. It was there, under all of the yelling and anger."

"I will."

"No, you won't." Returned to my back.

"What does that mean?"

Tell him? Tell him I knew the whole story: his mother, his father, his aunt? Probably not. But then, at that moment, he said something. His sentence hit me, physically so. Stopped my heart. Jammed down my throat. Lowered my temperature.

"It's not only about my name."

He knew. And he knew I had interpreted his message. I had followed the trail to its conclusion, which seemed to lead me a little closer to him, if only because he trusted me. Even so, in that very instant, I felt somewhat frightened, like when a child and I thought a ghost haunted my bedroom closet.

"No?" I answered.

"No. There's more to it. Let's just say there won't be another Mrs. Alworth. This, I can promise you."

"You don't have to say such a thing to make me feel better."

"That's not what I'm doing. You told me you knew why I agreed to marry you. Guilt, you said. Not entirely wrong, but not entirely right. People may think I'm selfless. No one ever asks what I might get from this marriage. And I do get something. You've given me quite a gift, Amanda. In the years ahead, no matter where I am, when people ask if I have a wife, I will say, 'I was married once. She died young.' They might say, 'You should marry again.' I will tell them, 'I can't. I can't.' And they will leave me be. And they won't think anything of it. I'll be the poor widower. Nothing will seem strange to others. I won't be forced to meet someone's sister or someone's friend from school. People won't whisper about me. I'll be left by myself. I'll be a perfectly normal person. A perfectly normal person who had some bad luck. You've given me a good story. I plan to keep telling it. Maybe I can live a little bit ... a little bit ... I don't know. Whatever it is, I'll get to live it alone. Not so selfless of me, is it? I'm just as manipulative as you think you are."

A long, pensive beat.

"I'm glad I'll be of some use after I'm gone," I said.

He laughed a sad laugh, one directed at himself, as if he understood all at once: *How pathetic am I?*

"I'm fine with it, Orest. Except the alone part. I'm afraid I don't understand, but I don't think I'm meant to understand."

"I've never thought that part of my life was meant to work out. Let's just leave it at that."

"I won't pretend to know what you mean. I wouldn't want you to be alone, though. I could've been alone these days, but I'm not, because of you. You frustrate me and drive me mad, of course. But you haven't left me alone. I would like to think you deserve the same."

"It's complicated."

"Who's condescending now?"

"It just is."

We could have ended there for the evening. Like the prior night, I had more to say, for better or worse.

"I realized something today. I sometimes wonder what I'll miss, if the dead ever miss anything. I think I'll miss finding out when I'm wrong. That's another way of saying I'll miss learning."

"You want me to ask what you learned, correct?" he said.

"Correct. I've always focused so much on acceptance. I had to. I had a lot to accept. Can't remember ever not accepting everything as it is. I also have no patience for people who refuse acceptance."

"That, I know."

"But I realized today acceptance isn't enough. I've overlooked something just as important. Probably more important. Forgiveness."

"Don't tell me you've found religion."

"It's not religion, Orest. It's … I don't know. I don't know why I'm even thinking like this. That's not true. I know exactly why. I suddenly want to forgive everyone. Every stupid, little grievance I've carried around with me. I want to be forgiven, too. Let it all go. It's so heavy. It shouldn't be so heavy, this life of ours."

"Are you trying to tell me I need forgiveness?"

"I think you need both, Orest. Acceptance and forgiveness. We all do."

I folded over, away from him, toward the windowsill. Nothing more to say.

CHAPTER TWENTY

Orest

The after-bedtime sounds clattered in my head. Eight o'clock each night, my world, inside those walls, under those sheets. Had a talent, I learned. I could turn noise into pictures. I could see my aunt, my uncle, the help, all of them talking, laughing, in rooms tinted bright. I took with me the gray and gloom, the cold looks, the short words. Warm. Relaxed. Free. That is how they lived without me.

I never heard anything that clearly. The house, too big. Sometimes, rumbles and ripples, the way my stomach sounded after skipping a meal. Those topics would bore me, I guessed. Other times, bubbly fizz pops and horn honks. The happy conversations. The unhappy conversations, those I knew. Spouts of dragon steam blasted against the ceiling and under the floorboards. Train-whistle screeches and mad-dog woofs. More and more of those each week, each month.

Clonks up the stairs, I heard late one night. Clownish clonks. Should have been asleep. If anyone had found me awake, punishment, for certain. I put my talent to the noise. One of the maids struggling with a heavy laundry basket? Uncle hopping and hobbling on that bad ankle of his? Closer. The clonks got closer to my door. Not a game. An intruder? A monster? Squeezed the top of the blanket into my fists, jammed it under my neck.

The handle jiggled. The door opened. A picture frame around a purple shadow with tree-branch arms and rubber middle. My aunt. Something in her hand. Not sure what. She swayed like a marionette with tangled strings. Tripping, but never quite falling down. I sat up, said nothing. She usually told me straightaway what she wanted. ("Get up early tomorrow. Don't be late.") Not then. She took her time. Walked in, like she'd never been there before.

"You, my boy, are bad luck. You know that? You have to. You know everything. Came to tell you anyway. Bad luck. Wanted you to know. That's it. I'll go."

Shooting through a mouth crusted with black-red oil and wax, her words, the flavor of broiled medicine and hot-summer swamp. My eyes watered.

"No questions? You've got so many damn questions. So many damn questions all the time. Not now? Why not now? You don't want to ask why you're bad luck? You just know? You know everything and you have so many questions. That's your problem. Fine. I'll go."

Not her normal talk. Her words, typically spoons of salt or sugar. Precise. She always used a different voice, an accent people with money must have bought at school. Not then. The sound of slush on the road after snow, gunk in the throat when sick. The ink from each letter smeared into the next. She headed for the door, thank goodness.

"No." She stopped. "No. No. I'm going to tell you." Index finger pointed up, she drew a circle in the air. She turned around. "You should know. A boy should know. You are bad luck, because your uncle and I … Your uncle and I … I don't even know what to call it. You won't see much of your uncle. Don't see much of him now. No one does. No, people do. Some people. That's the problem. We're still married. Yes. Yes, indeed. We're still married. Have to be. Have to stay married. Nothing else for me to do. But he gets to do whatever he wants. That's the arrangement. Understand? We're married. He's not."

I nodded. I didn't understand, not then.

"No different than now. When he's away, he does whatever he wants anyway. Does it all. I used to go with him. Sometimes, I did. Do you believe it? All of his trips. Most of his trips. I stopped. He didn't want me around. Said I shouldn't come. You know why? Do you? You know everything, so tell me why."

I stayed quiet.

"You showed up," she said, like that man with the red jacket at the entrance of the carnival last summer. Loud and electric, her arm swooped across her body, her finger in the air. "That's why. No more for me. I had to stay here. For you. That's what he said." From strong to weak, from shout to whisper, she bounced. I could not keep track. "Found someone else to have fun with. Bet he's got a lot of someone elses." She twirled around and seemed to get dizzy. I pulled back, tucked my legs into my chest. Thought she might crash right down on top of me. She felt around the mattress and sat on the end of the bed. A glass. That was what she had in her hand. "Enough for me. Thought it was worth it."

She hunched forward. Never so casual. Sat like a man, her legs open, both hands around the empty glass. Stared into it, probably hoping it could refill itself.

"A lot of someone elses. How many do you think?" She seemed to want an answer. "You know everything. How many? How many is too many? How many until I leave? Three? Four? I would leave. I would." She got angrier, like I had disagreed with her. "You don't believe me. Damn you, I would. I've left people before. I still can do it. Don't think I can't. I can."

A gunpowder boom dying, then smoke. Finished? Was she? I stretched my legs out underneath the sheets.

"But I can't." She patted around the covers. Wished she would not find me, but she did. Grabbed my ankle. "Can't because of you."

Set her glass on the floor. *Remember*, I thought. *Remember where it is.* Could have knocked it over. Another reason for her to be mad. Over and around, her arms and legs splashed onto the bed. Too dark for me to make any of it out. I moved fast to the other side. Tried to get off the mattress, onto the ground. She trapped me, her arm around me, pulling me against her.

"Who'd take care of you? Can't go with him because of you. He won't stay because of you. Bad luck." Her left middle finger curved "S" shapes from the top of my forehead down to the tip of my nose, ending on my upper lip. Felt wetness at the back of my knees. Slap. Bite. Strangle. She could have done any of them. Her hot liquor breath blew in my face. I tried to match my breathing with hers, to avoid the smell. Exhale with her. Inhale with her. Could not keep up.

"You're not just bad luck for me. You know that, right? Not just bad luck for me. Ask your parents. But you can't. Bad luck."

She drummed the space between my eyes. "I'll tell you something you don't know. You know everything, but you don't know this." Held her index and middle fingers straight out, thumb up, like a pretend pistol. Pressed it to my head. "Bang," she said. "That's how he did it, your father. You always asked what happened to him. That's how. Bang, right to him. Did it himself. You know why? Because you tore right through your mother." She whacked my stomach, shaking it. "Killed her. She didn't make it. He couldn't stand it. Him. So tough. Nobody tougher. I don't think he gave you one look. Couldn't stand the sight of you. You took his wife, for Christ's sake. You took care of him, too. Bang. Both at once, you did. Bad luck."

Her hand stayed on my stomach, even lower.

"Just being born, that's your bad luck," she said, dozing off. Her words, not close together, each one farther and farther behind the other. "Just being born. I'll stick it out. Don't worry. I'll stick this one out."

Finished, I hoped. Fallen asleep, wrapped all around me, like a blanket I couldn't kick off.

CHAPTER TWENTY-ONE

Amanda

Christmas tree.

Two words. Harmless words, really. They never meant much to me. I did not become particularly excited when one went up, nor did I become particularly sad when we took one down. But the words, a reminder: everything ends. I did not need more reminders. The last night of August 1923. Around the dinner table, the conversation, innocent enough. September had arrived so swiftly, my mother said. This started a tabulation of events and markers that would follow in fall and winter.

"And the Christmas tree," Catherine said. "We've got to think about where it will go this year."

"She's right," my father said. "Looked out of place by the front door last year. We kept hitting it when we tried to get in and out. Maybe by the window this Christmas."

"The window would be nice," Mom said. "The neighbors could see it from the street."

Window. Door. I could have screamed, "I won't be here."

But I did not. Could have diagramed their insensitivity. Could have taught them a lesson in their own obliviousness. Instead, not a sound from me. The silence, itself, a truth: the absence of wanting.

No more holidays with the family. No more dinners around the table. My body could not afford them. No longer could pretend to eat. No more hiding everything from Mom. No matter. No one noticed. They watched me almost too closely. Too closely to see how far and how fast I had fallen. My cheekbones, razors up through my skin. Dresses floated over me, catching on barbed hipbones. A comparison. They required a comparison, maybe a photo from months earlier. They might have seen. But no one looked for a photo, one with health and aspiration cresting over the frame's edges. One so very different from the current picture.

Barely upright. I barely sat upright through dinner. No longer even wished to try. Just stagecraft to preserve my arrangement. No reason to prop up a lie, because I could not even remember why I ever bothered to lie in the first place. I suppose I once had wished for more from Orest. Comfort and consolation should not have been enough, but I told myself they were. No more room to trick myself. No more time to trick myself. No longer desired even our simple routines. Impossible, but true.

Nothing in particular—no single incident—altered my outlook. Orest and I had no quarrel. Exchanges continued pleasantly between us, as recently as the evening before. Pleasant exchanges. Those alone awaited us every night. Pleasant exchanges no longer seemed worth sitting up straight. Sickness would offer me no more, I accepted. Neither would my husband, if I even could call him that. Respect. Perhaps friendship. No more.

I had ingested every type of pain, all swished together as a single concoction, tasted in hourly mouthfuls. A peculiar tolerance, I had developed. No more pain, I believed, prematurely. With that Christmas tree, a new pain. One of emptiness, the deep ache of unfulfillment. Somewhere in my mind—in the back or in the front—I probably had housed hope. Always did, although I had fooled even myself on this point. Hoped I would get better. Hoped Orest would look at me differently. No, not my courage people admired, but my capacity to deny. Like those lumbering into the final stages, looking back over luck never discovered or chances never granted, I felt the absence.

The absence of wanting.

The meal over, at the entrance of the kitchen, my shadow stronger than my muscles and bones, I watched my mother tend to the dishes. "Mom," I said, the running water drowning me out. "Mom," I spoke more loudly, becoming lightheaded.

"Sorry, didn't see you," she said, taking my plate, slotting again into her domestic groove, so unaware.

I stood there for a few seconds. My mother washed and dried that single plate, unconscious devotion to her family in the torn-towel circle, exquisite and smooth.

I began to estimate my gratitude according to every clean item ever placed before me.

"Mom, I think I should come home."

Her actions hit a snag: relief at my return, but a return for a specific purpose. The statement went unacknowledged. She continued to the next plate, without interruption. Then, she stopped. Set it all aside.

"Are you sure?" she asked, struggling not to tip her preference.

"It's time. It's just time."

"Tonight?" She approached me with caution, as if too sudden a movement could change my mind.

"Tomorrow. I'll tell Orest tonight."

My mother heard the resignation in me, the sound of a chamber filling itself with echo.

"And you were right, Mom," I said.

Right? How she probably longed for such affirmation, but not then and not like that. I clinked the first notes of a dirge. The weakness. The pathos. *An imposter*, she must have thought. *An imposter*. I met pronouncements of death at the earliest age with obstinacy, yet this somehow got the better of me. She hooked her hands into my shoulders, her eyes searching my face, expecting to catch a glint of irony. Instead, nothing.

Dad entered. "Everything all right in here?"

The triviality that could have followed, my mother likely feared and hated. She shut the cap tight on the conversation, saying, "Amanda told me she'll be coming home soon."

"Why?" he asked, so honest, so amnesic, so typical. I sometimes adored how miscast my father appeared on a stage directed by others, an actor from a comedy inadvertently roaming onto the set of a fevered drama. His presence managed to turn the plot, usually for the better.

"It's just time, Dad."

"Orest," we heard Catherine call out from the front door.

"Please don't mention anything," I said. "I'll tell him myself, tonight."

"Of course. Of course," Dad assured me as he exited.

I followed. Mom took my hand, anchoring herself on her right leg, holding tightly, so that I could not slip away. I leaned toward her, loosening our tense, joined limbs. "I'm fine, Mom. I'll be fine."

Unconvinced, she let go.

"Good to see you, Orest," Dad nearly shouted in the living room, his overcompensation covering him in conspicuousness.

"Captain. Hello." Orest dropped his voice for my mother, as he still had no comfortable form of address, adrift in the waters between Mrs. Bannon and Margaret.

"You've eaten," Mom said.

A question? A statement?

"I'm fine, thank you."

The characters I had scripted, speechless before me: the awkwardly chipper father, the aggressively protective mother, the unsuspecting husband. Would not do.

"We should head back," I said.

"We can stay if you would like," Orest said with only a polite amount of sincerity.

"Yes, you can," Mom said.

"No. It's getting darker. I'm tired. I'll be back tomorrow morning."

My mother hugged me as if her arms and pressure could cure me right there. She whispered, "You can stay now." I patted her back. She released me, grudgingly and finally. A quick, hard squeeze from my father and I was out the door with Orest. Our last evening walk? Perhaps. The edges of the air, crisp with approaching autumn, the taste and smell and chill of pure joy. I loved it all, with no connection to memory or expectation. Only the sensation of that single moment.

"I think I interrupted something," Orest said.

"What? No. After-dinner talk."

Distracted, of course. Wrestled with *what* to tell him, as much as *how* to tell him. Regardless, how would he react, if at all? His detachment always threatened me. He held the ultimate advantage.

"Tomorrow's September," he said. "Hard to believe."

His initiation still pleased me, even after those months, even with half my cells bloodless and dying. "We said that at dinner. It happened so fast."

"Your birthday is in September," he continued. So nonchalant, he blended the observation with the unlocking of the front door. "September twenty-fifth."

Such a whirl, his mention of my birthday. Almost dizzy, as if I had spun for hours on an out-of-control amusement ride. "That's right. How did you know?"

"It's not all run-over-there, stop-that and break-it-up." He shifted to the side, letting me enter ahead of him. I looked around inside Aunt Cecilia's house. I thought I might have crossed into the blurred familiarity of a dream, with an oddly slanted ceiling, out-of-place chairs and curious colors on the walls.

Orest split from his pattern, walked right past me, into the dining room. He called out, "I thought we might do something." He returned. "Maybe we have your family over here. Maybe for dinner."

"Here?" Less a dream, more a prank, perhaps.

"I'll talk to your parents. Maybe tomorrow."

Tomorrow? Tomorrow, Mom and Dad expected me to come home to them. This, I could not tell Orest. I did not want to tell him. "Tomorrow then," I said, heading up the stairs.

"I can't believe it's September," he said. "Almost a year. I've been here almost a year. Goes by quickly."

He was deaf to his insensitivity, blind to how slowly I moved, to my weakness. He looked beyond it all, as everyone did. As I dressed, I struggled with an unco-operative body, with the possibility I might have to disappoint my mother one more time. A refreshing unease, really. A thrilling discomfort I had considered lost, only hours earlier. In the room, Orest spread out his blanket on the floor.

"We could go to a restaurant. Elizabeth, Tom, Catherine, your parents. I could take us. Maybe Childs again."

"No, not necessary. I wouldn't want you to have to do that."

"We'll see what they say tomorrow."

He turned away from me.

Wanting, not entirely absent, not yet. A somewhat familiar anxiety returned. A temporary phenomenon? I did not care. Everything was temporary, for the sick and for the healthy, for those granted weeks, for those guaranteed decades. I fell asleep wondering how my husband and I would celebrate my twentieth birthday, wondering how I would explain to my mother the prospect of spending another week in that house, perhaps more.

CHAPTER TWENTY-TWO

Orest

Lost myself in that "O." Might as well have stood for obsession.

Sometimes, I would imagine it wrapping itself around me, like a rope, tightening and squeezing me unconscious.

Other days, I would imagine tripping over its edge and falling into the opening of a hole without a bottom.

A disc thrown at me, spinning and spinning, bashing my head.

Why not an "X"? An "X" is the same as an "O." Just as anonymous. At least an "X" carries action. A cross. A stamp. The "O" sits there. Blank. Negative. I could see the loopy, loose wrist writing it out. I wanted the swift strike of the "X." Felt trapped by the "O." Rather have been smashed by an "X."

I dreamed about my parents. Two ordinary adults living in an ordinary house, nothing as large as the house where I lived. Their faces, I likely took from a couple I once saw on the street when out with the help. Probably a nice couple. Probably smiled at one another.

I kept them with me, stored them, let them out when I needed to see what could have been. I could not bring them out any longer, not after what my aunt told me.

"Couldn't stand the sight of you. Would never give you his name."

Bang.

New dreams. Dreams of my father at the end. A man's face, fuzzy at first. A change in the room. Fog in the corners, the news drifting in. Everyone finding out at once without anyone saying a word. The man's face, suddenly older and ugly. A fairytale villain.

"What's his name?" a woman would ask.

"Michael Alworth."

"A junior?"

"Not a junior. A murderer."

No murderer would be his junior. The "O" took care of that. A single letter to keep me apart from father and family. He declared, "I will not claim you. You are not mine." Worse than the death, this namelessness.

Never would I be a prideful Junior, like some boys in school. The "O" somehow blocked people from giving me much of a name at all. If my aunt ever called me Michael, she did so only as a last resort. To others in the house, Master Alworth. To my uncle, barely seen, simply the Boy. Once in boarding school, I became Alworth. Some even attempted to cut it down to "Al." Never caught on.

Rarely did others call me Michael. Not permitted by me. I would scowl at whoever used the name. Point made. The person would back off, go back to Alworth. I felt undeserving of that, too, but I had to be called something. Just never Michael.

I learned about matricide when we studied Aeschylus.

Fourteen or fifteen when it happened. I liked literature. Not as much as history, but better than other subjects. I often skipped books or browsed the first few pages, faking my way through classroom talks. I expected to do the same when the teacher assigned Aeschylus. No, not quite. The plot sprouted claws and climbed into my head. I looked off the page, left to right. Anyone there? Anyone watching? I half-expected to see Aeschylus, leaning up through the centuries, saying, "This is for you." Orestes, the boy who kills the mother who murdered his father. Aeschylus taunted me, filling in the lines of my story. No father. No mother. From a long-dead Greek playwright, my identity. I had found my "O."

Spring of 1914. The visit home on a break from school would be my last. A visit to an empty home. My aunt had taken to traveling on her own in those days, trips conveniently timed to coincide with my returns. Before heading back to campus, I packed my bags, as usual. No one noticed their heaviness, because no one noticed much about me.

One final stop: the never-enter room.

Bad places had become normal and safe as I aged and grew. Not the never-enter room. The double doors, still powerful and menacing. My hand shook before I touched the knob. I looked over each shoulder twice, worried someone miles away, states away might appear. No amount of oil could silence the hinge squeak. My steps vibrated a little, then died, as if the sounds had passed right through the furniture, the walls. An unnatural place. Over to the filing cabinets. Which one? Did not remember which one. I pulled and thrust, pulled and thrust, drawer after drawer. Maybe my uncle had moved it, removed it. Finally, there: my birth certificate, all that mattered to me in the house. They could keep the rest. Outside the never-enter room, free.

Weeks after my seventeenth birthday, when the other boys ran off from the school year to families happy to have them home, I walked away. The letter. I had timed the letter's arrival for when she would have expected me. I wrote several drafts. Some hateful. Others remote. I finally wrote:

> I want to thank you for having taken care of my needs over these years. I find I no longer can impose on your generosity. I believe you have prepared me to assume a life of my own. I will write to let you know what happens. Please let me know if I ever can repay the kindness you have shown me.

Ungrateful, I expected to be called by my aunt. At best, ungrateful. Probably worse names, but names, at least. Better a malignant character in her life's story than unnamed. I worried I could hear what she would say, no matter how far away I moved. Her snake-rattle in my ears, next to me in bed. I had given her exactly what she desired: liberation. More than liberation, an excuse to wallow. "I was wronged," she could complain. "Wronged! Fill my glass!" A drink for each person who had wronged her could drown a city.

Straight from school, into the army. I talked my way past questions of age and consent. No one cared, as long as I looked old enough. Again, there, I became only Alworth, a word usually snarled by officers. ("Alworth, at attention!" "Alworth, stop lagging!") This aggression, I enjoyed. For too many years, disdain floated toward me. Implied, never asserted, edging out enough territory for denial. I never questioned my place in the army. Effect had a cause. The anger brought me alive.

One night, my full transformation.

"What's your first name, Alworth?" one of my bunkmates asked.

"Call me Orest."

I spoke tentatively, although I had rehearsed in my head for weeks. I studied the room, worried figures from my past—my parents, my aunt—would ram through the door and drag me back into namelessness.

"What the hell kind of name is Orest?"

The comfort of an insult.

This, I felt I deserved.

CHAPTER TWENTY-THREE

Catherine

We held my sister's funeral on September fourth. She died on September first. Or she died late on August thirty-first. I want to go to the cemetery after they make the headstone, because I would see the date. A doctor or nurse must've known exactly when she had died. But I couldn't ask my parents. When did she die? When did you find her? What was it like? Was she still in bed? I don't know if I'll ever learn the answers, so I at least would like to know if Amanda died in August or September. I want to know if I should start feeling really sad at the start of every August or if I could wait until September.

I know that on the morning of September first, Mom waited and waited for Amanda to come home for breakfast, until she could wait no longer and went over to Aunt Cecilia's house. I heard my mother later tell someone, "I sensed the end with every step."

I don't know what it was like for her when Mom saw Amanda's body. I think she was still in the bed, so she passed away in her sleep. Some called that part a blessing, as if how my sister died made us feel better about the death. I don't know what my mother did, how she got word to Dad, if they brought in a doctor to look at her, how they got her out of the house. I don't want to know. As much as I would like to be treated like an adult, I don't want to deal with whatever it is adults have to face.

When I'm older, I'm not sure which day I will remember more: the day she died or the day of the funeral. I probably will think of Amanda as all of September. Or all of September and part of August. I came home from school and knew something had happened by how hard my mother hugged me. It felt like she was trying to hold me so tight, so I'd never die, because maybe she'd not held Amanda tight enough. I didn't see Dad cry, but he looked different, like he'd been left outside in the rain overnight. I cried so much the first day, I thought I'd run out of tears. I cried as much the next day, maybe more. I don't know where all of the water came from. I thought I would've been empty.

I don't know if Amanda ever had thought about her funeral. She never discussed it with me. She never discussed much at all with me. I almost got to the age when she would've told me things, when I would've told her things, the way you do with an older sister. She probably did think about her funeral, because she thought about everything. But if she hoped it would look a certain way or if she wanted us to do certain things, she hadn't told us. She might as well have given the ceremony a you-deal-with-it shove across the table before she walked out of the house one final time. I think I said goodbye to her that last night. I think I hugged her, too. I'll tell myself I did, even if I didn't.

There was a mass, like the one we had for Aunt Cecilia. None of it seemed much like Amanda. She had her own style, but we were too tired and too sad, I think, to try anything different, so we did the same as everyone else. Probably why every funeral resembles every other funeral. Families are too tired and too sad to do anything different. Neighbors and police officers and teachers from Saint Vincent's and people from Saint Barnabas spread out among the rows, so Saint Columba's seemed full. Not as full as on Christmas or Easter. Probably more people than Amanda would've expected.

We sat in the first pew. Mom had her hand over her chest the entire mass. Maybe it would've cracked open if she hadn't held it together. Her eyes were a pond in the early morning: wet and still and dark. Elizabeth looked so old. She aged a decade in days. I could read the hurt in the lines of her forehead, which were never there before. Her hair pulled back, her face scraped of glamour and smiles. I wondered if I'd ever see her smile again. She was all I had left. The next time someone would ask about my family, I would have to say, "I have a sister," not, "I have two sisters." I could explain, but no. No.

Dad on one end and Tom on the other, I sat between Mom and Elizabeth. We locked together, all limbs and sags and slouches. We had become one bruised, limp being. In the same pew, separated by a few feet or more, was Orest. Straight and stiff, pressed and combed, he didn't seem distressed. In fact, he looked like he attended a different ceremony. He was a tall, polished statue. We were ashes.

Nothing from the ceremony seemed to affect him. I saw it, though. I think only I caught it: a blink-and-you-miss-it smile across his face. I wondered if he thought of some memory of Amanda, something she might've said to him and only him. "You know, my funeral is the most important day in our marriage," she might've told him. "Without it, you never would have agreed to this. We had to make sure I would die before we could get married." Sounded like something Amanda would've said. And it sounded like something that would've made Orest smile, even for a second.

Like with Aunt Cecilia, we went to Holy Sepulchre after the church. I started to think like a child, like I was four or five years younger. I hated it, but I couldn't stop. Too tired. I thought about how glad I was Amanda and Aunt Cecilia were there together, so they could keep each other company. I started to think of how cold my sister would get in the winter or how wet in the rain. I hoped putting her in the ground could be like planting a seed. In the spring, I could go back to get her, fully regrown. I hate that place, what it made me think, what it has taken from me, what it eventually will take. Whatever I have to do, I won't end up there. I know I should want to be there with Amanda, but I can't.

We returned to our house after the cemetery. The mourners spread throughout the first floor, taking in food and handing out condolences to Dad and Mom and Elizabeth and me. Even to Tom. People paid special attention to me. I could tell some didn't think I understood what had happened. I absolutely understood. Amanda was alive, got sick and passed away. They must've forgotten how old I was. Doctor Caputo told me how smart my sister was, how she would've made a great doctor, how maybe I should consider becoming a doctor, too. I have to think about it. Not just yet.

No one talked to Orest and he didn't talk to anyone. No one really knew who he was, how important he was. He was the widower, after all. At a different funeral, everyone would've gone to him first, not us. But he seemed happy to have no one bother him. I saw him walk into the kitchen at one point. He came back out only a few minutes later and headed straight for the front door. He didn't stop to say anything to any of us. He just left. I watched him through the window. My father was out there, too. The two of them spoke for a little while. Dad did most of the talking, from what I could tell. I wondered if maybe Mom had asked Orest to find my father and bring him inside. Except Orest turned away and began walking down the block, away from us. Dad came in and didn't say anything. I thought maybe Orest would return after a little while, that he might've needed air or had to get something from the precinct.

But Orest wasn't coming back, at least not that night. And when that sunk in, it made me realize all over again that Amanda was never coming back. And I was so tired I started to become so sad. I had to go right up to my bedroom, so no one could see me cry.

CHAPTER TWENTY-FOUR

Orest

"Your name won't be on it."

That was what the Captain told me. My name wouldn't be on the headstone.

"It'll say Amanda Bannon, not Amanda Alworth. We thought it best. You've done enough."

He said other things, too. About no longer walking through Lincoln Park on his way home, because she sometimes would wait for him. About not being a good enough father, because he did not understand her. About appreciation for what I had done. I cannot remember the details. I do remember what Mrs. Bannon said to me in the kitchen.

"She loved you, Orest."

Those words hurt. Could feel them in the nerves of my teeth. Nothing quite like it for some years. Some women I have known could hurt worse than any man. Mrs. Bannon, now among them. I had to get out of there. Thought I had made my exit, until he nabbed me. Hollow and wasted, drooped shoulders and dark eyes sinking into his skull. Remnants after a typhoon.

"Your name won't be on it."

The sentence jabbed into me. Out oozed resentment. Resentment? Why? Toward whom? The Captain? Even more troubling. Below all other feelings on the day, resentment should have been buried. But I could not dismiss it. The resentment churned in me. I did not understand. Only felt it. I had to avoid them. All of the Bannons. I had to be alone.

Back to Cecilia's house. No claim to it, no longer a son-in-law. I wasn't even a boarder. More like a trespasser. A trespasser at the funeral. No mourners approached me. No condolences offered. Just whispers and stares. Whispers and stares. A trespasser in a house, at a funeral, in a family.

"Your name won't be on it."

What you tell a trespasser. I planned to vacate as soon as possible. Not on this day, though. Nowhere else to go, to stay. A practical reality, nothing more. Once inside, the drag of days-long ceremonies began to lift. My collar loosened, my neck turning more easily.

"Your name won't be on it."

Why? Not why would they keep my name off the gravestone. Accepted that. Why did it bother me? Preoccupy me? Free. Finally free of obligation, right then and there. Free from the be-home-late and dinner-with-my-parents exchanges. Free.

Over to the dining-room table. I sifted through copies of the *Newark Evening News* from the last few days. Amanda usually had collected them, disposed of them. Pulling the paper from the steps became the first task assigned to me without her. Annoyed me. Supposed to have less to do without her, not more.

Where was it? I had not bothered to check before. Her obituary. No reason to read it. I had heard the news at the precinct the morning she died. The details—the where, the when—all came out later. Nothing needed from the paper. I needed something at that moment, though. Missed the listing on the first review. Settled down. Calmed down. Page-by-page. Line-by-line. There: Amanda Bannon. Resentment again watered my mouth. No Amanda Alworth on the headstone. No Amanda Alworth in the *Newark Evening News*. No Amanda Alworth anywhere. My eyes twitched, reading every word. My knuckles clamped hard, tearing into the page. No reference to me at all. "Beloved daughter of Joseph and Margaret." Yes. "Cherished sister of Elizabeth and Catherine." Of course. Even Tom made his way into the piece. Not me. Absent. Edited out. No reference whatsoever.

"Damn them," I said out loud, slapping the paper on the table, pounding it three times with my fist. The *them*, not the newspaper staff. No, the Bannons. "Damn them." The sound boomed. Over to the door. Would not stop until I found them. I would let loose a storm. Lightning and hail. I turned the knob with my left hand. My right arm pinned the frame in place. Opposite commands from each side of my body. My reasonable self took hold. No. No. Banged my forehead against the back of my right arm. No good. No good to come from it.

Did not want it, I had to remind myself. My name on her grave. No. I would have swatted it away, if asked. Sneered and swatted. Maybe some nasty, do-not-even-think-of-asking-me-again remark. Not then, with her gone, the house empty. Only outrage. Outrage over what? A personal insult? A show of disrespect? To what? The marriage? Pride? Maybe it was pride. Or perhaps not. I peeled from the door, fell into the couch. Did not matter. Amanda Alworth. Amanda Bannon. Only words.

Words on a page. Her life, reduced to words on a page. Days earlier, she walked and breathed in that very room. She rested now only in a series of paragraphs and narrow columns in a single edition of a newspaper. No brown hair and grayish eyes and splotchy skin. A font, a description. Unjust? Maybe to some. Not to me. A fate that awaited everyone, words on a page. The system deemed it so. A system, not to be surmounted. A birth certificate. A death certificate. Maybe a marriage certificate. Words on a page. All most human life ever could hope to become.

"What's my middle name?" I had asked my aunt.

"You don't have one," she told me.

Only words on a page. Held it in my hands then. All I was to the world. All I ever would be.

I never told Amanda that story. Other stories, but not that one. So many people asked about my name.

Only she pointed right to Aeschylus. She knew. Clever girl. Should have seen then. Would I have let her call me Michael? Maybe. Eventually. How many more days would she have had to hold on to reach eventually? At a funeral, I suppose, one buries the eventually. Hated that. Why? Why had I held back? Amanda wanted it. Cared about it. "Can I call you Michael?" Why not yes? I wanted someone to know, if honest. More a secret than the name itself, that I wanted someone to know. Choosing Orest, a dare. Sean? Theodore? No intrigue. "Nice to meet you, Sean." Ends there. Orest was a challenge. She accepted. I declined.

The house grew dark. The newspaper, the day to be put behind me. Walked upstairs, past her bedroom. Our bedroom? No, just hers. Again, a trespasser. Back to my first room. Not back to the bed. Not just yet. Stages. First, the room. After that, a mattress, perhaps. My body had become more accustomed to the floor. On the ground, relief initially. No middle-of-the-night trips to the bathroom. No questions to answer. A full night's sleep. No rest, though. No sleep. Funerals disrupt patterns. Right? Not enough will to push myself to sleep.

The breaking morning harassed me. Had I slept? Could not tell. Certain stretches felt more like suspensions of consciousness, not actual rest. I prepared for work. I could make as much noise as I wished, with no one to wake. Still, I moved carefully. What was my routine before? Could not remember. I had one. We had one. That one, still fresh to me. The old one, harder to locate. Outside, the early autumn air teased me. Cold and warm at the same time. Felt very little, though.

At the precinct, awkward consolations and greetings. No direct condolences.

"How's the Captain?" they asked.

"Don't expect him for a while," I told them. "It's hard. Harder on him than he expected."

Him?

Thought I could return to my before-marriage days. Like putting on a forgotten article of clothing packed deep in a closet. Wrong, though. So wrong. Such a misjudgment. That life no longer fit. Had Amanda refashioned it? Taken in some parts, let out others? Even at work, a place she never touched. Supreme confidence in everything I did there before. Something different afterward. The idea I belonged elsewhere, itching behind my ear. Scratched it. Kept scratching it throughout the day. So distracted. No emergency, I hoped. No emergency to test me. Not ready.

Out of the precinct, a trackless locomotive down Pennsylvania Avenue. She did not wait for me. No one did. Did not matter. Seeing the house in the distance relaxed me. Spotted something. A note on the door: "Orest, please know you are welcome for dinner. You are family. Joseph and Margaret."

I crumbled the paper. How could they? Slammed the door behind me. Why? They thought I cared to join them? I was family? Family members are in obituaries.

They were there. I was not. Obituary people go to dinners in a home.

Over to the dining-room table, back to Amanda's words. Nothing there not noticed before. My absence, even more galling. No "Wife of Orest Alworth" in print. She would have wanted it. She would have. Yes. Not "Wife of Orest Alworth," though. It would have read "Wife of Michael O. Alworth." Perhaps the *Newark Evening News* would have listed Orest in quotation marks. Amanda Alworth, she would have wanted. Micheal O. Alworth, I would not have wanted. One desired, one avoided. Neither there. Would it have been so bad? "Wife of Michael O. Alworth." I probably would have raged and roared. Another reason to hate the Bannons. Had it risen to hate? No. Still resentment. Strange, regardless.

Why not? *Why not*, either regretful or impulsive. So regretful then. Impulsive before. Why not marry her? Sure. Why not insist on her using the name? Regret. Another eventually? They added up. Michael. Amanda Alworth. Would have cost me nothing before. Cost me so much afterward. A bill that could not be settled. Anything worse than a bill that could not be settled?

A bill. More words on a page, this bill. Lines and digits, expenses and totals, all that was owed. I was owed. Owed a place in the obituary, at the very least. A bill from me to Amanda would include what? Inconvenience, certainly. Inconvenience counted in lost days, nights on the floor, tiring questions. I could picture it: "Amanda Bannon owes Orest Alworth a sum for the inconvenience of being her husband." What sum? What was the balance? Balance, as if more to this transaction than my expenditures. Something from her to me? Her bill? No. Paid well in advance, in surplus, on our wedding day, on the day I agreed to the wedding day. Nothing from her, except freedom. Freedom from speculation.

"Why's a man like you not married?"

"I was once. She died young."

"I'm sorry. Poor boy."

That would be it. I could go on living. That was what she gave me. Nothing, but freedom.

Also, missing. Missing, such a foreign feeling. There, nevertheless. I missed her. No denying it. I missed her. Such a typical reaction. "I miss my wife." Not to me. Novel. Entirely novel. Had I ever missed anyone? Not my aunt. Not my uncle. Maybe some of the help. Maybe a few men from the army. I missed Amanda. I thought I did. That escaped the newspaper. Could have been the headline: "Amanda Alworth— Missed by Her Husband."

Words on a page cut down every life.

Exactly.

I moved about the first floor with mad electricity, a severed line jumping and dancing in the wind. Opened and closed drawers, looking for blank paper, something to write. Found them. Sat at the table. Scribbled all of my Amanda memories. The stories about growing up with her sisters. Her peculiar observations about the neighborhood. More words. Her life would add up to more than a few lines in the *Newark Evening News*, more than government-issued certificates. I would make it so.

On page after page, every remembrance of her. No format. Sentences ran and ran. Housed it all. Housed all I knew of her. If I had hesitated for a second, even to organize, the flashbacks could have faded. Could have been gone, drained down the sewer, just like her. Gone.

Did not move from the table, feet fastened flat to the floor. A fountain, my memories in the early hours. Slowly, a trickle. Twenty minutes. Thirty minutes. Almost an hour passed without writing a word. Sleeplessness, piled so high and heavy, smothered me. A reasonable person would have seen as much. I did not resemble a reasonable person. I was angry and this anger made rest impossible. Would not let go of that pen until my mind had emptied.

The sunrise finally stopped me. Had to leave for work. Had to separate myself from the exercise. My attention stayed behind. My body, so disciplined. My instincts, so attuned. Ran through the rituals of the job. My head fixated on one word: forgetting. Was I forgetting her? Already? Forgetting the exact sound of her voice. Tried to play it back in my mind. Not right. The pitch too high, the "R's" rolling too long. Someone else's voice out of her mouth. Each night, farther away from my time with her. How elastic is memory? How thin does it stretch before it snaps, hours and hours heavy on its weakest point? Existence in memory.

Existence is memory? Forgetting her was removing her, like me from the obituary. Words on a page.

The end of the workday sent me rushing to the house, back to the *Newark Evening News*. My eyes owned each letter of the article. A difference. Needed to find a difference. If the words had changed, reality had changed. But nothing had moved. Each "A" stood in place. Every period clung to the back of its sentence.

I could not tolerate the static page. Everything around the words had continued to evolve, all life, all activity. The more time passed, the more the words became history, a history I could not rewrite. I picked up the pen from the night before and crossed out the "Bannon" after "Amanda" in the paper. Above it, I wrote "Alworth." A hacked, inelegant pairing, but some relief. Had done all I could. Righted the past, at least in my own mind, at least in one edition.

Up from the table. Behind me, I left the newspaper, the sheets of scrawled memories. I went up the stairs to the bedroom with a dull satisfaction that nagged at me. *Amanda Alworth*, I thought to myself. If only in one edition, she would be Mrs. Alworth.

Not the first.

The awareness tripped my heel, slugged me in the stomach. Mrs. Alworth. Another Mrs. Alworth had made her way into the paper. April of 1897. I had put her there. Clasped my left hand against the bridge of my nose. Blood and guilt through my body. Could not even reach the bedroom. Fell backward against the wall, slid down, slumping on the ground. Sleep, not even a taunt. A joke.

Two Mrs. Alworths. Two obituaries. I was responsible for one. Without question, I was. My aunt told me so. Tore through Ellen Alworth. My destructive birth, a truth that twisted around me, growing as I did. The other Mrs. Alworth? Did neglect speed the end? Did it? Not the disease itself. Could I at least have slowed the downturn? Perhaps. If I had let her call me Michael, could that have helped? Given her another six months? A name for six months. A name for a week. A simple exchange. Too much to pay at the time. A bargain, though.

Two Mrs. Alworths.

"She loved you, Orest."

Mrs. Bannon had told me as much after the funeral. Not a direct blow. No. So much worse. Set within me an explosive device, not to be tripped then. Tripped later.

"She loved you, Orest."

The sentence was a laceration. I dug my knuckles deep into my temples, rocking back and forth, crouched on the hallway floor. Amanda may have loved me. My mother certainly did, if only the promise of me. Maybe the only women who ever would. My gift to those who loved me? Killed one. Ignored the other.

Amanda was right. Clever girl. Right about so much, but especially about the guilt. I had married her out of guilt. Penance in a fancy dress and some vows. Penance in the keeping up of appearances, some nights on the floor of her bedroom. The reward? Peace, I hoped. And freedom. Guilt begat guilt. A deed driven by guilt only led to more. Never to lessen, not on that night or any other.

Morning clubbed me once I walked outside. I expected my body to chime the September air that blew through me. Another day ahead of me? Unconscionable. Twenty-four unconscionable hours. A light schedule for some of them, thankfully. Desk work. Sat down to finish it.

Every minute stroke, so fat. An uneventful day finally sputtered to a conclusion. Held on until the last second, snorting, scratching. The clock finally hit its hour, releasing me to the streets. Get to the house. Had to get to the house. A side-to-side stumble down the sidewalks. Something in front. No note. No. Amanda? Closed my eyes tight, opened them. Catherine sat on the stoop. She smiled, even a few days since burying her sister. She smiled.

"Hello, Orest." Up from the step, she leaned in for a hug, her arms around me.

"Catherine." Nothing else from me.

"We haven't seen you."

"Work." Continued walking up the stairs, undeterred.

"Come to dinner tonight?"

"I can't."

"Tomorrow then? Or just come over for a game with me. Or I could come over here."

"No. I have to go inside."

Door shut behind me. Could not be bothered. Not then. My shirt, dark-patched and sticky with guilt. Finally inside.

Why did I come here?

Amanda had asked me. "Why did you come to Newark?" Whatever my reply, not enough, not true. I could not let her know the real answer. Was there a *real* answer? In a hazy, hypocritical head, what made one thing more or less real than any other?

I moved to Newark to bury Michael O. Alworth.

Was that it? So dramatic, but real. I assumed real. Newark, the only place on earth that would challenge me. Orest Alworth living somewhere else, what did it matter? Orest Alworth somewhere else could have gone about his days. What would that have achieved? Escape? Yes, definitely escape. So appealing once. Had asked for it almost every night. No more aunt and her house and her summer-swamp breath. Away from it all. To what? Where? I wanted what was denied me. Wanted to reclaim the street corners and parks and city noise taken from me. Orest Alworth, roaming those street corners, walking those parks, hearing that city noise. That Orest Alworth could live anywhere, maybe even forever. Every move—military-to-police, small department-to-large department—led to the return. My return, my reclamation. A victim of fate, no more. Wrong. A victim of fate until the end. The end?

Around the house in the smoke of loss and weariness, something greater than ambition pushed me, pulled me. Drove myself into the couch, skull into the cushions. A victim of fate until the end. Marrying

Amanda, my fate. A step on the way to fate. No? Yes. I dropped to the floor with a noise no one heard.

On the ground, fast, rough spasms in my limbs, seizures and quakes. My marriage, a footnote, a plot deviation to throw readers, fill pages? No. Not a footnote, but the next chapter. Final chapter? The final chapter in a drama, a drama written in incomplete birth certificates, marriage records and obituaries.

Some antagonists spill blood. I spilled words.

Words in death notices. I had put them on the page. How many words had I spilled? Had to know. Turned on my stomach, drilled my knees and elbows as I made my way to the dining-room table. Threw up my right arm, steadying with my left, I felt around the surface without looking, snatching down the newspaper. Fell to my back. After a few breaths, I held Amanda's obituary in the air above my head, counting each word. Lost track a few times. Started over. Frustrated and burned, I tossed the paper to the side.

So many words. So many words.

Ellen Alworth. Amanda Bannon. I wrote them all. Some artists work in verse or paint or clay. I practiced the art of the obituary. Amanda crept into my mind with that observation.

Michael Patrick Alworth.

Wrote his as well. My father, a ghost story told to me by my aunt. My father, a menace, an idol, a villain, a savior. Never could connect with one of those. Stuck to the floor, the evening hours sliding by, my father adopted a figure I finally understood: widower.

Father and son, our wives lost while young men. The similarities stopped there. Any comparison, forced. The loss, the idea of loss, seemed true regardless. The absence looked almost identical. Some blank spaces, deeper and wider than others. The nothingness overwhelms. Mike Alworth, without his spouse. Me, without my spouse. He lasted only hours. I lasted days. An intolerable pain and a fast strike—*Bang*—ended him. For me, a contusion, a contusion that spread, threatening to hemorrhage.

Envy. In those minutes, I envied my father.

Certainty. Mike Alworth at least had certainty. No surrendering to the floor, day after day, pondering options. Not one day. My father knew he could not last one day without his wife. Debate ceased. The moment taken into his own hands. My father did not writhe in a slow hurt. Misfortune showed him his purpose. Clarity when he put the gun to himself.

I began to admire him.

"You're just like your father."

Damn whoever said it. Wrong.

They were wrong. I was nothing like my father, never more so than right then. No laying himself out, prostrate to providence, for Mike Alworth. He would have beaten me for my display, shaken me by the neck for my cowardice.

"No wonder I didn't give you my name!"

Certainty. Mike Alworth had certainty.

I wanted certainty. My entire life, no certainty.

Finally.

"Why did you come to Newark?"

To end it.

Conclude the tragedy. Write the last chapter. Add the final words to the page. Ellen Alworth. Mike Alworth. Amanda Bannon. Orest Alworth. One more obituary to author. A sweetness soaked my mouth. Soreness behind my eyes, jittery at the unburdening. No more days. Not one more day of it for me.

I moved with lightness up the stairs to the bedroom. I searched for my gun. The enormity actually calmed me. Determination tightened my actions. Paused a few seconds. Where? Turned myself around in a circle. Where? Over to the door, to the room not visited since Amanda had died. Another never-enter room. Cold and stale. Would I leave the same scent? A different one, one of dried blood and rotting organs? Loss does have a smell. I sat on the bed. Never did that with her.

My eyes all around, over to the doorway. Would not walk through one again. So many things not done again. Walking through a door. *Bang*. Gone. A never-exit room. Everything packed into those walls. Every minute of it all, crammed into a snug space, carried off and wiped down. Just like that, I would be forgotten. I first would have to be remembered to be forgotten. Not the right word, forgotten. What was? What was the right word for someone there so faintly he was not enough to be forgotten?

Stop.

All of it would disappear. Not only walking through doors. Not only the inconsequential. The bad. My aunt's house. *Bang.* Gone. Her in my bed, liquor-breath in my face. *Bang.* Gone. No. She could not be my last thought. Not my aunt. She had too much of me all along. If she were in my head at the end, I could go back there forever. Back to her house. Waking up in that room again. Had to have new last thoughts.

I shook my head, neck side-to-side. Index finger and thumb to my eyelids.: *what-could-have-been family, first day in a uniform, marching in formation, phrases …*

Amanda and her phrases. Blame and choice and forgiveness and acceptance. Good-enough thoughts in my mind.

Barrel to the head. Pull the trigger. Barrel to the head. Pull the trigger. My body swayed back and forth with the recitation.

Heavy. The gun felt heavy. Never quite as heavy as then. Tired. I was so tired. No other reason, but I could not remember the gun ever feeling quite so heavy. Lifted it from my lap, up a few inches. Tried again. Only seemed heavier. Torso clutched, I got it to my head.

Nothing.

I waited. Thirty seconds. Thirty more seconds. I counted: *one, two, three …*

Still, nothing.

Another thirty seconds: *one, two, three …*

Nothing. I heard nothing.

CHAPTER TWENTY-FIVE

Margaret

I only could do the waiting.

Not even six in the morning. Did not expect him, but there he stood, at the front door. Saved me the trouble of walking to Cecilia's to evict him. I intended to do it by no later than eight. When Catherine had come home crying the night before, after he had treated her so cruelly, I had enough. Only Joseph's persuasive powers kept me from going there right away. He said I should hold off until the next morning, probably hoping I would have changed my mind overnight. I had not.

When I looked at Orest, I ran through what I had planned to say. I would have told him how he did not deserve my daughter, how Amanda had wasted the last months of her life on him, how he would have broken her heart all over again with how he had behaved toward her little sister. I would have thrown him out of our lives for good, forced him to leave Cecilia's house that minute. But I could not do it. I told myself Amanda would have wanted me to show him some kindness, no matter what the price to me. That is what I told myself. Maybe I was just too weak to let him know what I really thought. Or maybe I judged him the weaker one between the two of us. And to unleash such anger on him would have been brutal. Perhaps that is my role in this world, for my strength to appear like weakness, so the weak can appear strong.

He stood before me without a sound, a stray animal searching for shelter. Instead of telling Orest what I thought of him, I closed my eyes for a few seconds and asked, "Would you like breakfast?" He nodded. That was it. He came into the kitchen and sat at the table. I poured him coffee. He wrapped both hands around the cup. It shook when he brought it to his mouth, like he never before had performed such a simple act.

"My first name is Michael," he finally said to me. "Did you know that?"

"Like your father?"

"Like my father."

That was all he shared right then. When he finished eating, I told him to go upstairs and lie down in Amanda's old room, on her bed. He slept through the morning and into the afternoon. I did not wake him for dinner, but he came down not long before we were to sit. He said he would leave. We insisted he stay. Six chairs around the table, with one empty. Maybe we had kept it open for Amanda. Maybe for Orest. I did not know.

He took the seat. None of us made any noise for a few minutes, until he said, "I'm sorry, Catherine, about yesterday. I was not myself."

"I understand," she said. "I understand."

During that dinner, talk tottered like a table with a missing leg, with *ummm*-s and *hmmm*-s, with questions about Tom's office and the precinct, with none of us caring about the answers. Orest remained for about two more hours after we had cleared the plates, then he returned to Cecilia's. Part of me wondered if we ever would see him again after that evening, that he might run away in the middle of the night. We saw him at almost every dinner. He continued to stay in the house. No one ever mentioned to him the idea of moving elsewhere.

On Christmas of 1923, he accompanied us on a visit to Holy Sepulchre, the first time we had been back there. He later told me how he had found himself among all those who ever had cared for him: his mother, his father, Amanda and all of us. *Good for you*, I thought, *but my daughter is still dead*. I did not say this to him, of course.

By March of 1924, the Newark Police Department had named Orest a sergeant. Not long afterward, he came to the house one morning, after Joseph and Catherine had gone for the day. Told me he had to leave the city, move somewhere else. He could not explain why exactly. Something he had to do. Asked if I could help give the news to Joseph, not unlike what I had done for Amanda, almost exactly one year earlier. My husband took it hard. He drew some consolation from the fact Orest had enlisted in the New Jersey State Police.

Joseph had to set aside his projected dream of Mike Alworth's boy rising through the ranks of the Newark Police Department. But the image of him as a member of a new unit began to take prideful shape in his mind.

"Orest is with the Troopers," he told everyone.

I was not sad to see him go. I had grown accustomed to having him around, yes, but I needed him to leave, for my own sake. I could not grieve Amanda with him there. He reminded me of her last year. And I wanted to forget that last year. I wanted to remember my daughter before he ever had walked into our home.

After Orest left Newark, I did not think we would hear from him ever again. Joseph insisted we would. He was both blind and deaf when it came to that boy. I wanted to tell my husband, "Don't get your hopes up." But that would have started a fight or hurt his feelings. I could not bring more sadness into his life. Even worse, if Orest had contacted us, I would have had to listen to Joseph remind me how wrong I had been.

For months and months, we only could wonder what had happened to him, with no news coming our way. Not even a postcard. If you had asked me to guess, I would have said not much ever would change for Orest. He would drift from town to town every few years, never quite settling down. He might meet an unfortunate end, either on the job or by his own hand, without our home to rescue him.

Maybe I was wrong. Maybe one day, a fellow Trooper would invite him to dinner. Orest would follow a piece of paper dotted with directions to a town in the central-southern divide of the state, down streets lined with large trees and manicured lawns. He would be welcomed at the door by the Trooper's sister, caught in some enchanting laugh. He would feel the way Amanda did when she first saw him. The sister would have a name, like Evelyn. He would say to her, "Call me Michael." He would tell her about his first wife, what he had done for her, which only would make Evelyn love him more. They would marry. Maybe they would have a daughter and name her Amanda. When older, the daughter would ask about her name and he would tell her about his first wife. As his daughter would grow up and have her own family, they would hear of her father, who took pity on a dying girl and agreed to marry her during the last months of her sad existence. They would pass on the story, from generation to generation. And my daughter would live on as a blank, secondary character in another family's history.

The idea made me furious. They would not know her. She would become theirs, but she was mine. She was mine long before she ever was his. And she really never was his. Orest had become the hero, a lie that sickened me. Those in the future would know nothing of her. Only that—for some reason none of us ever understood—she wished to be the wife of an uninterested man in the last months of her life.

Why had she done it? I had asked myself that question every day. Not so much anymore. Amanda must have thought she was in love. She only had the beginning. I would not say the beginning is the best part, but definitely the easiest. Maybe it was better that way. She never did see what love becomes. The disappointment and sacrifice and boredom and resignation. As I look at my husband, at my two remaining daughters, I have come to believe what we think of as love is nothing more than something so singular. All of it, our own, of our own making. Nothing quite as uniquely ours as the compromise we call love.

This something so singular is why I have remained where I do and why I always will, until they put me in the ground, next to my daughter.

Made in United States
North Haven, CT
08 April 2022

18008266R00136